The Last Kosovo Serb Won't Leave

This is a work of fiction. The characters and dialogue are products of the author's imagination and are not to be construed as real. Any resemblance to actual persons, living or dead is entirely coincidental.

© copyright 2007 by Susan Southworth

First Edition

Frozen Conflicts Books

The Last Kosovo Serb Won't Leave: A Balkan War Novel /Susan Southworth

ISBN: 978-1-4196-6263-8
Cover and book design by Susan Southworth

Except for fair use in reviews and/or scholarly considerations, no portion of this book may be reproduced, stored in a retrieval system or transmitted in any form or by any means, electronic, mechanical, photocopying or otherwise, without the prior written permission of the author, except in the case of brief quotations embodied in critical articles or reviews or scholarly considerations.

contact: frozenconflicts@yahoo.com

The Last Kosovo Serb Won't Leave

A Balkan War Novel

Susan Southworth

1

Kosovo January 6, 1999

Petar Bebic Cajkanovic walked higher into the woods than necessary. Winter's frozen mud was better than spring for walking. Spring thaws loosen the hard ground. It oozes and puddles. Finally it flows into streams of mud, rivers of mud. Not yet. Today he could hike for miles on firm mud. So he strode on though he had passed many young trees that would do for Yule logs. It was a good day, this Badnji Dan, a good Christmas Eve.

Frosted twigs and branches shone in the few weak shafts of January sun. Only when the light was fading did he stop and chop a small lopsided tree. A gust of wind from the mountain blew fine crystals of ice against his weathered face. He read the warning of snow and hurried down to the field where his winter wheat slept. His sled waited there, piled with wood. Its smooth flat bottom skidded quickly behind him, with barely a tug on the rope.

The old house was already deeply shsadowed by the Cruel Mountains when he took the last turn by the stream. At the stump he stripped the trunk below the top branches and chopped it into four—three Yule logs and the spindly top for Leposava's strange fancy.

She was in the warm kitchen, washing an old dinar coin to bake in the Bozic bread for Christmas Day.

Petar kissed each piece of wood before shoving it into the stove. He crossed himself three times. "As I kiss the Yule log, grant the cow, calves; the sheep, lambs; the broody hens, daily eggs; the oxen, strength before my plow; my Zeno, good health and Metohija and all the rest of Serbia, a peaceful year."

Leposava eagerly took the tree's crown. It was just the size for her childhood Christmas gifts—commedia dell' arte figures in costumes faded from jewel tints to muted gold, blue, pink, lavender and red. Her finger stroked the patchwork of colored triangles on Arlecchino's bloused shirt and tight pants. The acrobatic fellow was caught in mid-air, his knees and elbows cocked out either side. His red belt held a wood shaving, the weapon of his antic attacks.

Pantalone's mouth was invisible under a brush mustache and full beard made from broken bristles of a broom. On his head a Turkish fez, evolved from a baker's cap so Italians could mock the Ottomans. A frayed black cloak flowed over his hunched back, blue jacket and tight red trousers. Pantalone's wide belt held a moneybag stretched over one dinar.

Il Capitano's sword hung down below his boots.

According to her grandmother, beneath his military swagger was a coward, the Italian comic view of Spanish sailors.

The lovers' pale blue satin shone and gold still glistened on their sleeves and tasseled shoes. In their innocence, they alone wore no masks. They were the last figures she placed on the tree, giving them the leading role. Beside the tree Leposava lit two candles made with beeswax from their hive. At the base of each was a small wreath of dried oak leaves. She put an embroidered cloth and her grandmother's Sunday Russian plates on the sturdy pine table Petar had built soon after their marriage.

"We're in for snow," Petar promised.

Imprinted by her snowbirth, the white world drew her. Her mother and grandmother fled, barely ahead of Bulgarian invaders, birthing Leposava in the Cruel Mountains. Wrapped in an apron, then a sheepskin, they kept her warm between them. At the end of the war they brought her home. Their wagon was gone but their stone house survived the fire that destroyed other houses. It stood alone. Their Serb neighbors had been burned in their homes, killed in combat or simply vanished, never to return. The women lived alone in the valley for more than two decades. Riding pillion on an ox one summer Leposava held tight to Petar's chest, bringing a man back into the house with their marriage. Two generations of husbands had come as domazet into a woman's house.

"Snow brings winter dreamtime." There would be

snow in her dreams tonight no matter what the skies brought. Stepping outside, she felt the twitch of compression beneath her feet confirm his words. Twirling flakes obliterated the stars, the preamble of an all-night snow. It would blanket the mud by morning so they could go to Zociste. After Christmas mass in the monastery, they would break their fast with a lavish meal she needed to pack.

Brushing dried leaves out of the basket, she lined it with two napkins, then put in prune jam, cheese and dried pork. Bozic and hard-boiled eggs would complete it. Before setting out, she would heat up brandy and wrap it tightly next to small hot stones.

The kitchen was bathed in layered fragrances of oriental incense, young pine, burning beeswax and the fresh yeasty bread dough rising on the upturned pail beside the stove. The candles threw their dancing shadows across the wall. Arlecchino's black buttons shone and the bits of tin on Cherubino twinkled as the figures gently swayed on the little tree. The Yule logs crackled and hissed in the stove. A handful of straw beside each plate and nuts in the corners of the kitchen would keep away bad spirits.

They ate their supper of fasting beans. It was Badnji Dan and they kept it holy.

2

March 24, 1999

The Mercedes with a Swiss license plate drove onto the field. Inside five Albanians brandished Kalashnikovs with careless bravado while black ski masks hid their faces. Bogdan's face was bare, and he believed, recognizable to the teeming Albanians. Alone, he was an easy target in his Russian jeep. His Kalashnikov was out of sight, propped with its nose on the dashboard. He kept both hands casually on the wheel. With odds of five to one, he wasn't making any move toward his weapon. *Five to one visible. There are always more out of sight. The real odds are more likely twenty to one.* He'd survived enough ambushes to know the only way a Serb policeman stays alive in Kosovo is never underestimate the situation. His eyes stayed on the Mercedes and every weapon in it, ready to dive. As long as none of them touched a trigger, he could be patient. They were waiting, and he was waiting for it to begin. The deepening twilight bothered him. Night was merciless for Serbs in Kosovo. The option of being in a hurry wasn't his.

It smells like something's up. We don't want it going

wrong. They've got an ambush opportunity here, but they don't know how much support I might have in the van. On the road out of sight behind him was the van with four prisoners, four of their best captures from Djakovica.

What's the rush? Why didn't UCK go through their stooges, the KVM monitors this time? Last month they exchanged five elderly Serbs UCK kidnapped. KVM refused to even tell us where to pick them up. Those old people needed a friendly person speaking their language to receive them. Instead they were traumatized again. KVM could not grasp that. More likely, didn't care. All they do is spy on us for UCK to set up attacks and ambushes. This is better without that band of CIA spies and military advisors. Zoran says they gave their equipment to UCK, pulled out of Kosovo, and went to Macedonia for a while. Maybe its true. Why wouldn't they leave? They accomplished what they came to do—forced the YPA back in their barracks and turned over the positions to UCK. KVM's idea of a cease-fire is turn the province over to UCK. Bogdan inhaled the cigarette on his lip and crept forward toward the Mercedes. He edged out of gear with his right thigh.

A horse drawn wagon turned off the road behind the car full of gunmen. From the back seat of the Mercedes an arm waved it on. The wagon lumbered onto the field. The driver, barely a teenager, looped the reins of the two horses around the end of his board seat and hopped to the ground. The kid walked around to the back of the wagon and pulled off a mattress. He jerked his hand toward Bogdan's black Lada Niva. A white head rose from the bed of the wagon. The old man had a wide white mustache.

A second white head emerged above the side of the wagon. Her eyes found Bogdan. To return that gaze was hard. It was all he could do to keep looking at her. He felt shabby and worthless sitting in his car as this old woman, who could be his grandmother, struggled to climb down off the wagon. The kid kicked impatiently at the dirty snow, not helping the old couple. Bogdan ached to rush over to them, but one step without his AK-47 and he was dead. If he got out with it, the old couple would be dead first. This had to roll out. Any deviation was trouble. He knew how the adrenaline drove violence when fear and a hostile majority threatened a few of his police. Only intimidation kept them alive. But they had to stay calm and keep the level right no matter how bad it got.

Those two are lucky to be getting out alive. Remember that. Sit tight and stay alert, so this thing doesn't go sour. He looked into her eyes, willing her to stay alive and make it to his car. *You just have to walk over here and pray to God nothing happens, nothing jitters the Albanians.* The old man was down on the ground and she had one foot on a wheel and was reaching, reaching—. *I can't stand this. Every day it gets worse.* The old man took both her arms and pulled her down toward him. *They are doing it. They can do it.* They began trudging stiffly toward Bogdan's car across the shallow gray slabs of snow. *You can come. Just keep looking at me. Don't look back. Don't make eye contact with them. Don't try to ID any of them. Look here. Look into my eyes. Show me how much you hate me for not preventing this.*

The UCK prisoners left the van one by one, muttering in their slippery voices. He let their bent sneers roll off him. Passing Bogdan's window, the last of the four gave a wide snaggle-toothed grin of triumph. Behind him he stuck the finger though his wrists were still bound in the plastic cuff. *Those four have killed and will kill again! The kidnappers are getting what they want. What can we do?*

Bogdan evaluated the old couple's walking. They reached him but he didn't dare turn around or move his hands. Even as they were getting in the car, he focused intently ahead. *Easy does it.* The four prisoners got in the wagon and it left the field. Still the Mercedes held its piece of real estate.

"Are you both in? Can I start backing out? I have to go slow and not do anything to rile them. Make sure you're in."

"We're in," Petar answered hoarsely.

Bogdan lowered his elbow just enough to push the gear into reverse without letting his hands go out of sight on the wheel. He backed up until he was no longer in view of the Mercedes. Eager though he was to get away from the gunmen, he stopped and turned around to scrutinize his passengers. Their ruddy complexions, spider webs of lines around their eyes, deep creases across their foreheads and shallow lines on their cheeks recorded long decades of hard farming. He took the woman's hand and kissed it. "Thank, God." He patted the old man's knee. Shaking his head in mute disgust, he shifted into first and accelerated past the van. "Tell me how you are. Do you think anything is broken?"

Instead of answering, Leposava told him, "The village was guarding us. Everybody. It was no secret that they kidnapped us. They did not have to hide us."

"That's how it is. Two kidnapping attempts failed last night. Lucky for you UCK was in a rush to make the trade and get their prisoners out. They didn't have time to keep you overnight." *That gets nasty. Why the hurry? What's different this time?*

"Do you think they will come back?"

"Well, they got those four we traded for you. We don't have any more UCK prisoners here, so don't expect another kidnapping." He reassured them, knowing the kidnappings wouldn't end. "The doctors have to look you over before I take you home."

"It's late. I'd rather go home to bed," Leposava said.

"Shouldn't I take you to the hospital? I'd like to be sure nothing is broken." Bogdan glanced at the Lavazh Restaurant as he drove through Piskote. It was the favorite hangout for off-duty Albanian police from Djakovica. Besides the seventy in uniform, there were almost that many plainclothes Albanians who gathered intelligence. They keep the lid on Djakovica. The restaurant was blazing tonight and so full the Albanian security forces spilled out the door onto the street. *Looks like something's going down tonight. What?*

Petar looked at Leposava, "How do you feel, Zeno?"

"I'll be fine."

"We better go home," Petar told Bogdan.

It wasn't yet eight in the evening but Djakovica's streets were already deserted and ominously quiet as he sped through town. *What are the Siptari up to tonight?* On nights like this machine gun fire poured down from minarets. He was relieved to get back out in the country. It looked so peaceful. The moon illuminated snowy peaks on the Cruel Mountains above the dark mass of forests. Any policeman who was lulled by that beauty was a dead policeman. Bogdan was speeding now, as he always did to elude Albanian snipers.

"I woke with foreboding for today," Leposava told her husband.

"You were right, it seems."

"My dream of Djordje tortured me again. I lay awake and then morning brought Siptari."

"You must stop dreaming of Djordje. Those dreams fill you with tears and sighs."

Instead of responding to Petar, she only shrugged her shoulders.

The black countryside outside the windows closed

in around them. Bogdan wanted to keep them talking. "What road do you live on?"

"We're halfway to Prizren—off the road. We're two kilometers in."

"You don't have a road at all?"

"With no wagons to use it, the road vanished into the field. The forest closed in. We're safer without a road."

"I hope you are." Bogdan wanted to agree.

"They got us when we crossed the road. It's not safe to go wood-gathering over there anymore." Leposava's glance at her husband suggested a long running dispute.

Petar disagreed, "Winter is the quiet time."

"But ambush season starts again as soon as the leaves are on the trees. They booby trap and mine when they expect us.." *Why didn't they wait a month to get those guys out?* "We can't disarm them so they catch Serbs like you. But they capture and kill more Albanians than Serbs."

"They kill each other more?"

"They kill each other more than they kill Serbs."

"Why?"

"The clans compete. As soon as spring comes they are in every ravine, every thicket, bad blood in their eyes."

They had driven more than a kilometer out of Djakovica when the sky roared. An orange streak lit the night and exploded behind them. A monstrous ball of fire filled the rearview mirror. The police headquarters' six-story frame blinked out of a cauldron of orange. Bogdan stared in disbelief. Rahman had it built to tower above the city. Symbols of his power over Kosovo had to be visible and intimidating to all, even his fellow Albanians. He decided who got ahead and he wanted everyone to know it. Now it was burning up in a column of flames. *Who would do that? NATO is always threatening to bomb Serbs. Would they bomb one of Rahman's police buildings? His proudest achievements? Albanian judges, prosecutors and police who were removed for following the Kanun instead of Yugoslav law believed they would regain their power to make life miserable for others. They wouldn't destroy the seat of power they expect to recapture. All those Albanian police at Lavazh—safely away from the police building—? The world is too complicated these days. Who knows anything anymore?*

"More thunder. It's going to rain tonight. I hope we get home first," Leposava said.

Bogdan realized the old Cajkanovics had not seen the explosion. "I'll get you home in no time, Baba." He picked up his radio speaker and contacted the fire department. The police headquarters was hopeless but it could spread. His back seat passengers did not hear him.

"Oh, that was lucky," Leposava blurted out.

"Lucky, what?" Petar asked her.

"I saw a shooting star."

"No, there was thunder. You must have seen lightning. That's not lucky,"

"No, that's not lucky," she agreed.

"I used to go to a valley filled with oak trees. A single fallen tree would fill my sled as many times as I went back and forth, bringing it home all day," Petar reminisced. "That was fine firewood."

"We need our sled. It was full of wood," Leposava said. "We're getting close."

Tall pine trees pressed against the road and arched above, creating a tunnel that made this stretch gloomy even in daylight. "I don't know if we can see it at night." Bogdan slowed down with his high beams on. He swept his spotlight along the side of the road. Forest lined both sides until a rock outcropping. Where the forest reasserted itself, there was a narrow, almost imperceptible cleft.

"There it is." Petar said. The slab sled was barely visible under a low pile of chopped logs. "We'll get out here and walk back."

"Where's your house?"

"It's through there."

The opening was at most the width of a wagon lane. Bogdan considered whether it was too narrow for the Niva. "I've driven past here often and never noticed this slit." He turned the Niva toward it.

"I want to take my wood home," Petar objected.

"I'll tie your sled to the back and go slow."

"We won't see if any wood slides off."

Bogdan was not going to be put off from seeing them safely home. "I'll put the wood in back and pull the empty sled."

"The road's long gone. You'll get stuck."

"This goat can handle anything. I won't sleep if I don't see you home." He threw the wood in back, tied the sled to the bumper and started up through the narrow gap. The Russian jeep rattled as it hit the old ruts. Bogdan watched for stones and gullies. *Is there really a house back here?* The soft moonlight grazed an opening beyond the fringe of trees.

"Soon the melting snow will turn this into a sea of mud. You wouldn't be able to drive across here then," Petar sounded triumphant.

The mud may protect you more than anything, Bogdan thought.

"Today the snow was still solid and not deep. It was hard and good to walk on. The winds had smoothed it out for the sled. This was the day to go for wood to the far forest."

"Promise me not to go to the far forest for another year," Bogdan said as he reached their house.

Petar was grudging in his agreement, not wanting a stranger telling him where to get firewood, even the stranger who rescued them from kidnappers. "We don't go there more than once a year. It's only late in winter or when the snow and the sky are as they were today. That is the one day we go."

Petar and Leposava got out, thanking Bogdan.

"I'll go in and see if everything is all right." Bogdan stepped through their door ahead of Leposava, a drawn pistol in his left hand. The Kalashnikov was cradled against his right arm, his trigger finger at the ready. He walked briskly through the three timeworn rooms whose distilled fragrances tugged at his memory. They were old-fashioned like his grandfather's house when he was a child. Two hams hung from hooks in the large room and the loom had been used recently. He worried about them, but their life was so orderly. It was the way Serbs had long lived in Kosovo. *Maybe they will be fine back here.*

Bogdan loaded the wood onto the sled and followed Petar to his woodpile.

"Let me unload it onto the pile and take some indoors for you," Bogdan offered as he picked up two logs.

"No, let it wait for me 'til morning. I put the new ones behind, at the back, to age." Petar chose several logs from the front. "Come in. You need to have supper."

"I have to get back to the police station to file my report." He chatted on as though the police headquarters was not in flames. "I don't want to forget details. Anything might be important."

The wind howled like a she-wolf charging down the mountain. Petar shivered. "It has teeth tonight."

"Go in out of the wind," Bogdan urged. "Start the fire and get some liquids in you. I'll finish unloading the wood."

Leposava called out from the back door. "Please

come in for a coffee or brandy at least."

"I can't. Too much to do. Have a good sleep, Baba."

"I'll leave the door open. You can change your mind." Muttering to herself, she continued, "Always leave our door open Grandmother said, so guests can walk in."

Bogdan lingered near the woodpile, watching them through the open door to gauge how they were coping.

Leposava lit a lamp and put two logs in the last glowing embers of the stove. The stiffened bellows sighed before they gave out a puff to awaken a flame. "The house is as cold as if the fire went out days ago."

"It'll warm up soon."

"What are we going to do?" Leposava asked.

Petar was silent for long minutes. "We'll do what we always have done."

"They kidnap us to make us leave Kosovo. Now there are more of them because of the four who got out of jail. They can come take us again anytime."

"We can't know what they will do." He sighed and sat down heavily at the table. "We only know we have to have land to live. This is the only land we will ever have."

"With no Serb neighbors, we are too defenseless."

"You've always been here without neighbors. This is where you belong."

Leposava gave up. "Nije lako, ali ako." It isn't easy, but so be it.

"We'll stay away from the road. Bogdan said the road is dangerous for Serbs."

"A lot of thunder tonight."

That's not thunder, Bogdan knew as another rumble erupted. He loped around to the front of the house.

It's doubtful they heard his Niva retreat back down the narrow valley to the road.

3

Prizren, Kosovo March 24, 1999

Donald's arrival a few hours before the war began passed unnoticed. Nothing about him attracted attention—not the odd circular bag he carried, not even the absence of a traditional qeleshe on his white hair. Chatting comfortably in Gheg Albanian he was simply one more old man getting off the bus from Macedonia. Even the bored Albanian waiters from Café Oaza barely glanced in his direction as they leaned against a newsstand, smoking.

"So little traffic on the road today!" Agim stepped off the bus behind Donald.

After crossing into Kosovo, Donald only remembered seeing a boy on a mule, his feet almost touching the ground. Compared with the bare road of the journey, Prizren was full of life. Feathers and bits of fur clung to cages of chickens and rabbits on the sidewalk at his feet. Root vegetables in worn baskets lined the river wall. Terraces littered with minarets and medieval bell towers climbed the hills. The sights, even the air, heavy with exotic sounds and smells, all convinced Donald this was a place where anything could happen.

Retirement didn't define him here.

"And there weren't any checkpoints! I wonder why?" Agim paused to inspect turnips and onions.

"Checkpoints?" Noticing the Kosovo Albanian newspapers, Donald moved toward the newsstand. 'Serb Vampires' and 'Bomb! NATO, Bomb!' The provocative headlines were written in Tosk, useless for his linguistic research. *Where are they bombing? Sudan? Afghanistan? Probably Iraq.* Donald didn't try to keep track. At home his newspaper was the "Berkeley Weekly", when he remembered to read it.

Selecting three potatoes from a leather-skinned Serb farmer, Agim dropped them in his tote bag full of purchases from Macedonia. With a slight farewell, he hurried off to his home in Tusus.

Donald ambled in the opposite direction to the old Turkish quarter. Recognizing the name on the Serbo-Croat street sign, he turned up a narrow street and found the address of Cengiz' uncle on a gate. Inside the wall, the garden was untended. A gravel path lined with scrawny shrubs led past a shallow basin recessed in a cracked cement patio. A crumbled yeni turkce newspaper lay discarded beside a small table. The path continued to the imposing Ottoman house. Ornately studded metal doors glistened in the sun. The iron handle of the old doorbell turned hesitantly. Giving it a hard twist, Donald heard its peal echoing far inside the house. Minutes passed slowly before the bolt slid back with a solid clunk and one of the doors opened heavily with a faint scraping across the tile floor.

The crown of a dusty red fez emerged, its flaring black tassel bouncing above wisps of curly brown hair. Long tawny mustaches curled up in front of the old man's ears in the exaggerated manner of a Turkish pasha in a Rossini opera. Through thick glasses, he stared nearsightedly at the backpack tipping off his visitor's shoulder. "Ah! The professor of little Cengiz, yeah?"

Donald greeted him in halting Turkish, but Bayram continued in English. "Bayram Zonguldak. Welcome to my home. Professor Blythe, yeah?" Opening the door wide, Bayram beckoned his American lodger into his house. Shuffling his right foot ahead, he made slow progress in his soft slippers.

Hesitating on the threshold, Donald wondered if he should remove his shoes. Dismissing the notion, he followed Bayram into a corridor. At the doorway of a splendid salon, Bayram bowed slightly toward the opposite wall. "My benefactor." Under an elaborately nielloed Circassian dagger hung the gilt framed photo of his grandfather's cousin. Embroidered bandoliers crossed his shoulders and an ivory handled pistol was tucked into the long fringed sash wrapping his waist. He proudly held out a German carbine toward the photographer.

Climbing the stairs they entered a larger chamber.

Gold leafed calligraphy painted on glass and Turkish miniatures hung on the terra cotta walls. Niches held patterned ceramic pitchers. Silver platters and candlesticks lined a plate rack near the ceiling on three walls of the room. Wide divans flanking the slender fireplace were covered in kilims whose mellowed browns and greens showed their age. More kilims were nailed to the walls below the miniatures and covered much of the wide plank floor. The divans were lined with pillows covered in embroidered Turkish textiles. Wooden fretwork filtered the light and view through windows on three sides of a small table and two chairs.

"This is your room." Bayram caught his breath before adding, "not uncomfortable, yeah." He bowed his head and clasped his hands across his belly in a gesture of humility.

Donald used as much Turkish as he could, filling it in with Albanian, a far more comfortable language for him. "It's marvelous! Cengiz told me it is an old family home. I feel transported back to the Ottoman Empire." Swinging his arm in a sweeping arc, he placed his right hand over his heart in his approximation of the Turkish gesture of gratitude.

Still panting and red-faced from his labored ascent up the stairs, Bayram dropped heavily into a chair. With a nod he urged Donald to sit and poured two small glasses of clear yeni raki. "It was built by the fez." Abandoning his limited English, he told the history of his family's business in fluent Albanian. "Before I was born the shop produced the fezzes for Ottomans from here to Austria. Even Serbs bought some. Ataturk outlawed the fez and closed all production in Turkey, but we still had orders from Bosnia and Serbia. When Mussolini made the fez popular our factory had to double its employees to fill all the orders from Italy. By the time I inherited it, Mussolini was gone. Demand dropped every year. We began producing the qeleshe as a sideline for the new Albanian population. Thanks to Tito."

Donald had noticed the peculiar tall white caps on Agim and other men on the bus.

"The sideline grew to be our main line though we had some fez customers in Kosovo and Sarajevo. When the Albanians took over everything in '80, the fez business was finished. I was not sorry to sell, though my family in Izmir complained how little they paid. You can see the factory down near the river." Bayram tapped his finger on his nose. "They're selling more qeleshe today than when I ran the business. Albanian men wear them proudly. You'll never see a Serb in one, though all Serb servants were forced to wear them too. They revile them as a symbol of enslavement. But symbols can acquire new meaning." Sighing, Bayram fit a cigarette into his holder. Patting several pockets, he found his matches. "It's unlined, not like my fez. The white felt is shaped over a conical form and immersed in water. Almost anyone can make a qeleshe."

Bayram moved a small dish of pistachios to the

center of the table and set the matches beside it. Searching again in his pockets he pulled out two Turkish cigarettes.

Donald waved away the offer, intent on the effect of chewing a pistachio with sips of the sweet anise flavored liqueur.

Noticing he already had a cigarette in his holder, Bayram lit it. "But you didn't come to Prizren to learn hat-making."

Donald hoped to bridge the gap between Albanian and the ancient people who inhabited Albania. He nodded at the bag containing his dismembered bicycle. "I came for the Illyrian sites."

Bayram looked quizzically at the circular bag.

"My bike."

Bayram's inverted comma eyebrows flew up in surprise.

"And the local linguistic authenticity." He was thinking of spoken Gheg rather than Tosk Albanian in the most Albanian city in Kosovo.

"Authentic Siyakat?"

"I don't know Siyakat. Does it have vestiges of Illyrian?"

"Its not ancient enough for you. It's a form of Turkish in signs, codes and abbreviations. It was used by Ottoman administrators." Bayram added water to his raki, turning it as cloudy white as the mother of pearl inlay on the table.

"Why not regular Turkish?"

"Ottomans kept meticulous records of how they spent the Christian taxes, but would not want Serbs or other subjects to read them. The brilliant solution was Siyakat and I have the complete record of Ottoman construction in Prizren!" Bayram's voice betrayed pride in the old papers he had protected for decades. "Only I can't read them." He lifted both hands in a gesture of helplessness. "After the war a neighbor told me Tito wanted them destroyed. Because he was very old and too ill, he sent me to save the archive. Before he died he translated only a few pages. If he had lived, he was going to teach me Siyakat. He was the last man in Kosovo who could read them."

"Since you have his translations, couldn't the rest be decoded by anyone with a thorough knowledge of Turkish?" Donald minimized the difficulty.

"It is beyond me. I hoped Cengiz would help."

"I'd like to see them. Maybe the two of us could make some progress on the translation."

At this suggestion, Bayram's eyes lit up behind the heavy brown frames of his glasses and gold flashed inside his wide smile. "Please. Yes. Whenever you like."

An hour had swiftly passed in conversation when Bayram's housekeeper brought them a tray of small dishes and a platter of melon slices with goat cheese. They talked all afternoon like two old friends after a long separation. When the meat filled pastry triangles, smoky eggplant and shredded carrot salad in garlic mayonnaise had been eaten, Zeynep returned with baked dried apricots and clotted cream. Still they sat at the table, drinking sweet Turkish coffee in red striped cups without handles.

The elaborate fretwork fractured the old city's towers, minarets, and gilded domes into a mosaic. Prizren was full of possibilities and knowledge Donald wanted to pursue. "This must be the best preserved Ottoman city in Europe."

"The last city in Kosovo where Turks have influence. Other than Dragas and Mamusa, of course. But aren't Ottomans too modern for you?"

"I thought so." A side window gave Donald a glimpse of the market where Serb farmers were gathering their baskets and empty cages. They hitched horses and oxen to wagons and left as the shadows deepened over the river. Donald watched the light fading from his new neighborhood. Only the tile roof of a church on the high hill still held glints of the retreating sun. "I'm going to enjoy my two months in your house."

Bayram turned on the copper wall sconces and two floor lamps with heavy tasseled shades. In their warm glow the room was even more exotic and the divans more inviting after Donald's long day. He stared at them longingly and Bayram withdrew, murmuring, "Sleep well" through his own yawn.

On the first page of his notebook, Donald wrote:

March 24- retirement off to a very promising beginning. Bayram suggests I walk through Ciganska Mala, the old Gypsy quarter, unless it rains tomorrow. First I'll bicycle to one of the Illyrian sites. And I want to see the fez factory.

A light shower began to nuzzle the windows as Donald fell quickly asleep on his Ottoman divan.

4

April, 1999

Leposava still trembled at the first thrilling wail of Petar's gusle. Its undercurrent to ancient Serbian tales had traveled through centuries of pain. She did not think about the planting and weeding for her garden. Or the bread that needed baking. Or a drought that could come. Floating in the quavering remnant of Petar's youthful bass, she barely heard the right amount of water splash into the kettle. Without looking, she stopped pumping the handle and moved her good heavy iron off the stove. Setting the kettle in its place, she ironed the last fresh white curtain. The pressure of escaping steam warned her to lift the kettle before it could whistle and interrupt his song.

> "In the pleasant city Prizren
> Stephen, Serbian Czar, falls sick,
> Sorely sick, and like to die.
> When the Czaritza perceives this
> (She who wrote like any man)
> Quick she takes the pen, inditing

Three, four letters, and forth sends them
To Four quarters of the czardom,
To all provinces in order,
Duly calling all the lords.
'Hearken, ye our lords of Serbia!
Heavy sickness weights Czar Stephen,
Weighs him down, so that he dies.
Therefore haste to Prizren Castle..."

She let the tea steep through the rest of the story. Two cups patterned with gray twining reeds sat ready with a spoon on one of the saucers. The back of her hand lifted stray strands of hair off her forehead. Sighing, she smoothed her long brown print apron. The back door swung easily as she pushed it with her shoulder and went out into the mild evening. All day the sun had tried to pierce the fog and heavy clouds. A weak glimmer triumphed at last to cast a glow on Petar's face.

Leposava was startled to notice how worn his face was tonight. Several times since the kidnapping she had caught a glimpse of her invincible husband as suddenly old. His battered trousers hung loose, stiffened only where mud caked around his calves. Though still powerful, his square shoulders sagged. Even his proud white mustache seemed to droop. "With the sun on your face, you look like the Saint Nicholas fresco at Prizren," she told him, tenderly kissing his forehead. Setting his tea beside him, she added, "except for your cap."

Petar jerked off his square wool cap, freeing matted locks of thick gray hair. "If this is my moment to look saintly, I better take it." He licked the edge of the spoon. "Apricot." He alternated draughts of tea with the preserves.

"It's the last until I make more this summer." Beyond the stone wall, feeble rays of sun lit the orchard. The rainy month had delayed the opening of buds on the plum and apricot trees. "Did you hear that thunder?"

A gust of cold air swept down from the stone peaks of the Cruel Mountains. He listened, then shook his head. "I didn't hear any."

"More rain for my roses and your new barrel."

That afternoon Petar had finished shaving it down and fixed the hoops tight around it. It would catch more rainwater.

"It will wait 'til night comes." Picking up his short rounded bow, Petar began another song. His tough old hands so powerful in their instinct for farming were gentle in their artistry on the instrument that rested familiarly between his knees. At the end of the gusle's long neck, his left hand cradled the falcon's head he had carved when the century was young.

The new barrel stood beside the house. Fragrant curls of its wood filled a pail by the stove. The sheep were in their pen. The chickens were fed. The oxen had their hay. The day was over and they had used it well.

p 27 Medieval Serbian song recorded in G. Muir MacKenzie and A. P. Irby, *Travels in the Slavonic Provinces of Turkey in Europe, Volume I,* Daldy, Isbister & Co., London, 1877

5

April, 1999

Rain glittered on the windows of the Ottoman house day after day, forcing Donald to delay the fieldwork for his research. With so much rain the Illyrian sites would be too muddy. Instead he took up the Siyakat project. This was exactly the sort of problem he was used to solving with his ancient languages.

Cleaning and counting the old parchments took several days. Spreading them out across Bayram's long divans, they evaluated each parchment. After a week they had created a tentative catalogue. The lists of Serbian workmen's names and the amounts they were paid were set aside as unhelpful. The decoding could begin. Each parchment had its own sheet of paper where Bayram wrote down anything that came to mind as he studied it. Knowing the subject of the records narrowed the task. He soon recognized abbreviations of a number of standard Turkish words.

After preparing a short dictionary from the translation by Bayram's neighbor, Donald noted the forty most frequently used unidentified letter groups and symbols.

Abbreviations that looked vaguely Serbo-Croat, Donald thought might refer to local varieties of stone or other materials. Next he analyzed the structure in which the forty letter groups appeared and listed the terms that seemed likely to have been useful for the task. The signs and codes were the most elusive.

Cracking Siyakat was an enthralling game. Days turned into weeks as Donald helped Bayram with his old manuscripts. Only the soft rustling of a page taken up from its pile or replaced betrayed their silent absorption. The list of translated characters lengthened. A dozen documents had few unknown characters and they speculated on those, based on the context. His enthusiasm for their task increased as the construction details of Ottoman mosques, fountains and baths in Prizren emerged. The degree of centralized control from Istanbul to this remote corner of the empire surprised him. The work crews and craftsmen were local, which explained the many lists of Serbian names, but the architects were always from the capital.

Donald became so immersed in the Ottoman Empire, he barely thought of his own research. One day over dinner Bayram asked about his evidence that Illyrian was the source of the Albanian language.

"We have only scattered Illyrian vocabulary mentioned in classical texts. None of those words follow Albanian phonetic laws, so no one has made a convincing case relating Albanian to Illyrian." Wistfully, he added, "If only I can prove Albanians descended from Illyrians and, therefore, that they were here two thousand years ago."

"That is why they demand the rest of us leave Kosovo. They call us colonists."

"Even the Illyrians were immigrants. The Byzantines thought Albanians were immigrants when they wrote about their raids on herds of sheep. Once the Albanians appear in the area of Albania in the eleventh century, there are frequent references to them by Serbs and Greeks as well as Byzantines. Letters from the Despots of Epiros in northern Greece chronicle an Albanian tribe in a small neighboring territory."

"First no one sees them, then everyone does?" Bayram was skeptical. "That weakens your Illyrian theory. All the Albanian maritime words are Turkish, modern Greek or Slavic, suggesting they came to Albania rather late."

"Or it isolates them in the Albanian mountains."

"Over more than a thousand years, before their exposure to the Ottomans, they were unaware of the Adriatic Sea?"

"Well, yes."

"But the Illyrians were famous pirates on the Adriatic."

Unwilling to admit the point, Donald substituted another theory. "True, but the Thracians weren't. Bulgarian and Rumanian scholars identified more than a hundred

Albanian words derived from Rumanian. And there is not a single Old Dalmatian Latin loanword in Albanian. All the Latin traces to proto-Rumanian, so they had to be borrowed after the sixth century. That supports the Thracian origin."

"You might switch to the Thracian camp?"

"Not if I prove the Illyrian correlation." In his animated discussion of his research, Donald waved his raki in excitement, splashing a few drops on the carpet. Bayram's startled look stopped his flood of words. "Oh, I'm sorry. Did I spill on your carpet?"

"That's what Serbs do. It's no matter." Bayram's gaze shifted away from the floor. "I can't help with Thracian or Illyrian. The only loan words I know are Old Iranian."

Donald was startled, "Iranian words in Albanian?"

"There must be at least a dozen."

Each day while they worked on the Siyakat documents, Bayram remembered more Old Iranian roots in Albanian. It was an idle distraction from his real inquiry. Though useless in establishing a connection with Illyrian, one of Donald's notebooks was filling up with links between Old Iranian and Albanian. When the sun came out and the ground finally dried, he intended to work efficiently, making up for the weeks diverted to the puzzle of Ottoman script.

But when would the heavens stop pouring down on Kosovo? Rain had never been so abundant as it was that April in Serbia. Black and gray skies alternated. Wind howled and rain drummed as foul day followed foul night. The first spring leaves torn from their branches whirled past the window in a swarm of leaflets. Rain seeped in around the panes of window glass and under the door. Volleys of machine gun hail accented drowsy hours of steady drizzle. Slow motion dripping accelerated to furious battering. Some rain was so fine it was invisible. Too often it came in torrents, rattling down so hard Donald couldn't see the garden. It turned the narrow street into a canal, imprisoning him in the comforts of the Ottoman house. The world beyond the watery reflection of the salon remained unknown. The wet sky was indistinguishable from the rain-battered houses and earth.

  Rain did not thwart Bayram's Turkish housekeeper. Even in a downpour, Zeynep swam in from the soggy world to surface dripping in the hall, an amphibian with wet black curls circling her round face. At her neck blue beads glistened as brightly as sapphires. Setting down the market basket, she removed her rawhide sandals, and shook her hair, sending out a flying spray. She twisted fat handfuls of the pleats hanging from her wide hips, revealing the embroidery on her knee high stockings. Even after she squeezed out puddles of water onto the tiles, a trail of droplets followed her into the kitchen. The tiers of her long skirt stayed wet as fish scales for hours, weeping until the afternoon. Once dry, the high water marks darkened the fabric, recording the daily deluge.

For a month it rained on Bayram's well-run house. The kitchen came to life with Zeynep's arrival each morning. Pressed dates, stewing fowls, vine leaves for her dolmas, everything they needed from the outside world came in her market basket. She knew where to find virgin honey and the fattest meat. The quail awoke when she uncovered its cage and ruffled his feathers appreciatively. Coals in the stove glowed and roared under a stream of oil to brew the breakfast salep. It was the fragrance of that steaming drink sprinkled with cinnamon that coaxed Donald from the warmth of his divan on cold damp mornings. Barely pausing to tuck her sleeves high on her muscular arms, Zeynep started cleaning with mop, broom and dust rags. Her silent industriousness made the household function.

Laundry and ironing gave her most pleasure. With no sun, it hung in the kitchen, slowly drying in the stove's heat. When the rain relented for an hour or two, she rushed outdoors with her laundry basket. Donald followed the damp laundry out to the garden. Between the rains, the trees shed collected drops in a steady patter under a pallid watery sun. Lushly green and fertile from the downpours, the planting beds pushed up pale sprouts of Bayram's forgotten perennials.

Donald cleaned out the green scum in the basin. Fresh rainwater quickly filled it. Captured on its surface, the garden changed moment to moment under clouds or bleak sunbeams. Faint breaths of air refracted the image into an impressionist painting. Fond as he was of the struggling landscape surrounding him, the mirrored one transported him to an ideal garden or foretold what it would be when the sun finally shone.

The pauses in the rain were too brief for him to venture through the gate. Blackened clouds tumbled over each other threatening to unleash an impending cloudburst and chase him back indoors. Once Zeynep was assured her laundry was secure, she brought him tea in a tulip shaped glass with a dish of dates. She read the shiver of the trees so well; before the first raindrops fell she had the laundry hanging once more in the kitchen and Donald back indoors.

Zeynep's busy industry stopped only for her midday dinner. After she served Bayram and Donald, she ate alone in the kitchen. Though she was deaf, the patterns of cleaning, laundry and menus were perfectly established. Donald wanted to communicate with her beyond a smile or nod. Several times he tried to pantomime the rainy storms or his appreciation of her cooking. She watched him indulgently, rolled her eyes, then turned back to kneading her yufka dough.

After serving their late afternoon savories and sweets, she made the grainy Turkish coffee. Counting out twenty-four beans, she roasted them in a wire basket over the open flame. Transferred to the cool mortar and pestle, the hot beans shattered under her ferocious pounding. She cooked the coffee in a small tin-lined copper pot, stirring sugar in last before she poured it out, half filling the small cups. Donald loved the aroma. Even though he never had sugar in his coffee at home, its strong sandpaper blend of sweet and bitter became addictive.

Zeynep changed the water in Bayram's pipe, covered the quail's cage and went home through the rain. Sheltered in dry comfort, the old men chatted over coffee in the salon. Their early supper left long hours of evening. Eventually the unhurried flow of conversation lagged, its pauses filled by the fluid drone and excited flurries coming from the record player. Bayram took up his pipe, drawing thin blue smoke through the hose. The water gourd gurgled, mingling with the birdlike flute and throbbing darbuka. Immersed in his cloud of smoke and music with eyes half-closed, he reclined on the satin cushions of his divan.

The tyranny of bad weather kept Donald suspended in the contented Turkish household.

6

late April, 1999

The month that should have been devoted to Illyrian sites had evaporated. Instead, Donald had sorted, studied and translated records of the very Ottoman Empire remains that surrounded him in Prizren. As the records revealed their secrets, his curiosity about Prizren grew.

One afternoon the rain-swollen clouds were squeezed dry. Donald eagerly headed out to explore the neighborhood. For the first time he inspected houses that had been only gray blurs behind the heavy curtain of rain. Typically Ottoman, they were closed to the street, revealing little. The rich architectural rewards were only for the family within and those permitted to cross the threshold. This outward reticence was normal but the few decorative elements on the facades were curious. The oldest carvings on gateways and up high under tile roofs were Christian inscriptions, faces and figures. Even the neighborhood mosque had an unlikely bas-relief cross on the keystone of an arch.

As he climbed the hill, Donald imagined he was in the sixteenth century en route to the hamam to hear the latest news and scandals. The fantasy carried him to the door of the grandest baths in Prizren. The heavy door opened slowly, resisting his push. Inside the gloomy vestibule a man dozed behind a long counter. When Donald cleared his throat loudly, the attendant lifted one sleepy eyelid. Holding out a hand he accepted twenty-five dinars, pushed a towel roll across the counter and waved toward a row of cubicles.

Shedding all evidence of a twentieth-century American, Donald emerged shivering in the fringed towel wrapped several times around his bony frame. The sharp slap of too-big plastic sandals resonated on the dark passageway's stone floor leading down to the hararet. Light drifted from the grimy glass oculus at the dome's peak, softly illuminating marble arches circling the hall. Staying in the shadowy perimeter, he went to a small basin. The splashing reverberated like a powerful waterfall, breaking the empty silence. Scooping water in one hand, he splashed his face. A burly attendant lumbered over with a pitcher. Water spilled down Donald's shoulders, back and chest. The pitcher was refilled and emptied a few more times until he was thoroughly drenched. Unable to see with water streaming down his face, he felt himself lifted up onto a warm marble table. Then the massage and soaping began.

With his muscles quivering from the rough mitt's scouring, thumping and prodding, Donald stumbled out of the grand hall. He entered the hot room with steam so thick he could not tell if blurry shapes were columns or men. When it seemed too claustrophobic, he moved on to the bath of tepid water. The Ottoman genius for sequencing spaces led him through a series of rooms sampling a roman variety of waters of differing temperatures—running water, falling water, lapping pools, rippling sheets of water across the river of sleek marble floor. The final room was not a bath at all. Elaborately colonnaded and lined with divans, it was the resting room. Draining a bowl of cherry juice and honey, he lay back and closed his eyes for a long nap.

That evening, glowing from the Turkish bath, Donald strolled down toward the Bistrica River. Translating the signs on shops absorbed him. Posted on many were government stamped notices in Serbo-Croat asking Albanians not to abandon their businesses. *Why would they?* Prizren was full of commerce and crowds of people enjoying the best weather in weeks. Cafes lining both sides of the river throbbed with chatter and music. The Ottoman penchant for coffee houses had spread from Yemen throughout the Empire. Donald chose the whitewashed Cafe Oaza because it was full of Albanians. Tables near a television in the window of the bar were full. Only the furthest one was empty. Rusty from standing beyond the awning's protection, it was also out of the range of the kerosene heater. Accustomed as he was to San Francisco's climate, he didn't need the heater anymore than he wanted to watch television.

"Have I seen you here?" the friendly Albanian waiter asked him.

"It's been too rainy," Donald started to explain when his attention was diverted by bright lights that suddenly flashed on, lighting up the room behind the bar. Four men hunched over a table, laughing and slapping down cards in their game.

Turning where Donald looked, the waiter jerked his head at them, "It's the owner and his Turkish friends playing khedive."

Donald analyzed each syllable the waiter spoke. Wanting to keep him talking in hopes of picking up ancient linguistic forms in the local idioms, he asked, "How often do they play cards together?"

"Every night they are back there." Called to another table, the waiter cut off the chat. "Coffee?"

As dusk crept up from the river, Donald surveyed the city spread out around him. Red tile roofs climbed the terraced hills on both sides of the river. Horizontal rays of sun licked minarets and reflected golden in windows. Long shadows hid distressing modern compromises to the historic city, perpetuating the Ottoman spell. A scratchy loudspeaker's call to prayer challenged the faithful idling by the river. *If only I had spent some evenings here the past month, I could have heard so much Albanian. After my fieldwork, I'll come every night.*

A blue and black camouflage MUP group swaggered

down the tree-lined sidewalk, radiating invulnerability with every step. Between their black knit caps and body-armor vests, their square faces were splashed with paint, flattening their cheeks. Donald imagined their caps were migfer, the close-fitting Turkish helmets worn by Serbian Janissaries three hundred years ago. Sent on perilous campaigns, they subjugated new territories and kept defeated lands subdued. Each Christian family that refused conversion to Islam forfeited its first-born son. The boys were raised harshly in Anatolia, far from home, to serve as shock troops for the Ottoman Empire.

Today with the lowest birthrate in Europe, these young men were more likely to be the only children of their Serbian parents. *Did their centuries of repression influence this low birthrate? Had they become too pessimistic or acquired an oriental fatalism during five hundred years under the Ottoman suzerainty?* Donald left that to sociologists. He only wanted to enjoy the sunset and Turkish coffee.

Hoping to see the Zonguldak fez factory, he scanned the buildings on the south side of the Bistrica. Zlatni Papagaj Café could be a reflection of Cafe Oaza except its tables were filled with clusters of camouflage-clad men. Young Serb soldiers drinking along the stone wall flirted with attractive Albanian girls near Donald. Blaring speakers strung along the Zlatni Papagaj canopy obliterated all but broken fragments of their Serbo-Croat words. The owner's musical tastes varied from the hoarse mocking rasp of Milosevic rokeri to nostalgic Tito neo-folk tunes. Neither appealed to Donald.

His gaze drifted back to the hills above him. In an abrupt musical change a seven note minor chord opened a ponderous, unmistakably Russian piano passage in a narrow range. Donald's head snapped back around, abandoning his Ottoman daydream. The chords were familiar but he could not identify the piece. At the Zlatni Papagaj soldiers moved to empty a table for three pale, shorter young men. Their vests and ammunition belts were not like the Serbs and they had bandannas around their necks. One even wore a cowboy hat. It was obvious the new trio spoke a different language than the Serbs. Donald strained to hear their conversation. *What are they speaking—is it Russian?* Unsure, he was happy to have the moody music drive them from his mind.

"Rachmaninoff's B minor Moment Musical!" he blurted out, recognizing the theme.

Donald's outburst had been ignored, except by two waiters, who, misunderstanding, rushed over to him. Though wanting to prolong his evening at the café, another coffee would ruin his sleep. So he placed ten dinars beside his cup and strolled by the river. Swollen with weeks of rain, it was opaque brown with soil and rocks torn from the banks along its stormy route. The walls barely contained its rushing journey through the city. An old priest wearily shuffled past in his sandals. The sun left behind only dusky violet as it sank.

The twilight glow left the minarets and the bulbous dome of the Turkish bath. Beside him the Bistrica surged past unseen. Donald shivered as its cloying mist washed over him. It was time to go home.

The cobblestone street was deserted. Bayram's neighbors had retreated into houses dark except for light fringes around the heavy curtains and shutters. One group of windows glowed. Donald paused in the dark to enjoy the view of the handsome salon where his sleepy friend lay smoking his water pipe.

7

the next day

The warm spring dawn burst suddenly over Prizren, banishing the month of indoor confinement. Under a cloudless blue sky, Kosovo became a land that knew nothing of rain. Mule trails that had been too muddy to bike steamed and hardened in the sun.

Donald's camp kit was assembled and ready. At Bayram's door he almost reconsidered. The garden blazed with sun-soaked color, finally confident of spring. Sweet clouds of fragrance floated on a heat haze. Ivory syringa blooms released a scent of honey. Billowing lilacs tossed their heavy perfume at him. The quail sleepily basked in the balmy morning, tempting Donald to do the same. A lone Abu Hassan, painted mahogany red over golden fluted petals, emerged unexpectedly. The astonishing bloom was a relic of young Bayram's long ago arrival in Prizren with a trunk full of Turkish bulbs. The tulips had revived the war-worn garden and made him feel at home so far from Izmir. Reborn in the planting bed, the opulent Ottoman bloom outshone the rest.

Feeling the obligation of his belated fieldtrip, Donald

jerked the gate closed. His bicycle, finally out of its round bag and assembled, bumped down the sloping cobblestone street beside him. Behind the seat bungee cords secured his pack full of dry foods and his sleeping bag rolled inside a rain sheet. At last he would explore Illyrian sites.

"Does this road lead to a church?"

The language was strange, closer to Russian than Serbo-Croat. But the trio of young men approaching him was familiar, still wearing the red kerchiefs that distinguished them from Serb soldiers last night.

"Nyet." Donald knew there could not be a church up his street. Bayram's house was in the Ottoman quarter.

"What good is a road if it doesn't lead to a church?" Józik persisted. He was short and muscular, the most gregarious of the three.

Donald was so intent on identifying which Slavic language they spoke, he was slow to think of an answer in Russian.

"Znayu. In Metohija all roads lead to churches," a quavering voice answered. The stooped old woman was dressed in black except for the fringed shawl tied round her shoulders. Sweeping a trembling hand toward the hills, she told them, "The churches of a thousand years number a thousand. Look under every mosque, there you will find a church. The Church of St. Anna is under the Mustapha-Pasha mosque. The Church of St. Athanasios is under the clock tower of Emin-Pasha Rot. The Church of the Epiphany is under the mosque in the Maras-mahala. The Church of the Transfiguration is under the mosque of Mehmed-Pasha. Besides these are a dozen dozen churches. You cannot avoid a church in this city of Serbian czars."

Donald was taken aback by her archeological revelations. *That explains the crosses and Christian inscriptions on the Ottoman buildings. They were recycled from previous structures. Somewhere in Bayram's many parchments it must be recorded.* Prizren held too many diversions, pulling him away from his research.

"Are they all destroyed, grandmother?" wondered Valentin. "Did we come too late?'

"Ah, the Ukrainians have returned. October 20, 1944—I was there when you liberated Beograd."

"That was our grandfathers," Józik corrected her.

A striped market bag drooped from her arm. "Wait while I fill my empty bag with something to eat. I will show you as many churches and monasteries and hermitages as you can save." She shuffled off, still murmuring, "Under every Ottoman fountain is an altar. Under any Turkish bath is a monastery. The Church of St. Helena is under the last Mosque built by ... "

Across the river a Serbian waiter swept the stone pavement outside the soldiers' cafe. A voice from the past floated out of the speakers above him. The plaintive song drowned out the faint words of the old woman's mantra.

"Flow, flow, bitter tears!

Weep, weep, Orthodox soul.

Soon the enemy will come and darkness will descend

Woe, woe...

Weep, weep...

Starving people."

The voice of the legendary Ukrainian tenor, Ivan Kozlovske in the thin old recording prompted Donald. *Ukrainian, that must be it!* He expected to hear the music that accompanied the arrival of the Ukrainian mercenaries at the café. But this morning there was no Rachmaninoff and the aria was followed by Milosevic rokeri.

They watched in silence as the old Serbian woman returned. Saying nothing, she turned her head to look up at them sideways and beckoned with an arthritic finger for the boys to go with her.

"Do poba tchenia," the Ukrainians called back to Donald as they followed her up a cobblestone street.

Tempted by the old woman's knowledge, he hesitated. If he went after them, he would hear Prizren history to complete their knowledge of Bayram's Siyakat documents. Wavering, he debated with himself. His first month in Prizren had taken him further from the ancient Balkan origin of the Albanian language he came to find. All he had accomplished was a notebook filled with Old Iranian. Only his fieldwork could overwhelm that list and prove the Illyrian origin of Albanians. After that he'd be back here, writing it up in the garden. Almost six weeks remained before he was due to fly home. He'd uncover the ancient tongue and then explore Prizren. Someone else in the Serbian district would know as much as this old woman. Or one of the priests at the dozen remaining churches could tell him all they needed to know. He convinced himself there would be plenty of time to find someone when he returned to Prizren.

Resisting this new distraction from his Albanian project, he pushed his bicycle off toward the Illyrian sites.

8

May 1, 1999

The ravine's raw beauty enhanced the tempestuous music Donald chose for his field trip. Dark wooded slopes climbed steeply above him to aeries where only fairies and mountain sprites could dwell. Mists clung to rocky buttes that pierced the sky. Waterfalls plunged down sheer cliffs in their dizzy descent to the narrow ribbon racing toward Prizren. A mossy crevasse dropped off sharply only a few yards from his bicycle wheels. The mountain road twisted and turned, as it grew steeper. Exulting in the magnificent setting, he pedaled up and up. Not feeling retired at all, he convinced himself he was sinewy and tough, not old and thin. There would be a stunning discovery on this adventure, something no one expected him to find. That hope was encouraged by the realization he was exploring alone, except for a raven hovering protectively. A rumble overhead was barely audible over the opera in his headset. Thunder suited the dramatic setting. Donald was too pleased by the poetry of it all to fear an oncoming rainstorm. Not even Wagner saw such a romantic landscape of clefts and faults, precipices and peaks, as he composed the Ring. Brunhilde could emerge at any moment from the wild crags where eagles soared.

The shadow of a huge bird darkened the gorge as a cold wind swept over him.

"Hoyotoho! Hoyotoho, Heiaha! Heiaha! Heiaha," Brunhilde whooped in his headset as the earth shuddered. His bike jumped out from under him as a blast of energy sent him flying through a brown cloud that obscured the mountains. The headset, torn off his ears, took flight, replaced by a roar louder than Wagner.

He didn't remember landing on his pack. He couldn't see. He couldn't hear. His face was coated with something. When he opened his mouth to breathe more easily, it filled with grit he spit out. His arms and legs waved wildly in the air as he teetered atop his backpack. Helplessly marooned, he imagined himself the mock tortoise in Alice in Wonderland. The pride he felt mere moments ago in his vigorous ascent was banished.

Stop feeling helpless! How many Emeritus Professors could have biked this far up the mountains today? Echoes of the roar remained in his ears, replacing the lost Wagner. *Where is that headset?* Blindly, he moved his hands over the dirt and small bits of rock he could reach. The headset was not there. *Could it have blown over the edge of the ravine?*

Something softly brushed over his face and it was easier to breathe. A wet cloth cleared his eyes. He opened them on the soft moon face of a young man. Large gray eyes as keen as a falcon looked into his and full lips moved as though speaking. Instead of words, he heard swells and ripples. Donald started to speak but as he opened his mouth more grit fell into it and the first sound from his throat throbbed in his ears. Instinctively, his hands flew up to cover them. The glare of the sun emerging from behind clouds made him close his eyes again. *Where are my dark glasses?*

Suddenly he was tossed forward. His pack was pulled off. He bounced up, up, up. Every step hammered his stomach, as he hung from a giant shoulder. Squinting his eyes open he saw camouflage in all the colors of the mountainside pressed against his face. One of his arms dangled below him. On they raced up the mountainside. Another shudder struck the earth. Dirt swirled below them. The powerful arm gripped tighter around him. A large hand patted his right side as though comforting a baby.

At the top of the mountain they entered a dark passageway. Slowly Donald's eyes adjusted to the windowless gloom and he saw a packed earth floor below the legs of the mountain man. Lowered onto a board balanced on sacks of potatoes, he was finally upright. The earthen room smelled damply of men. A pine torch threw bursts of light on a low ceiling of branches and twigs framed in large timbers. Spitting and flickering, the torch's fragrant resin made Donald's eyes water.

Still dazed and deafened, he stared unknowingly at a basin of warm water with soap set beside him before he gratefully washed the coating of dirt from his face, hands and neck. As he drank a cup of warm tea with a hard biscuit, a welcome wave of heat washed over him. The pungent aroma of mushroom soup reached his nose before someone put a spoon in his hand. Its steamy warmth lulled him to sleep. The bowl was nearly empty when he slumped sideways against his pack.

Wild winds that had howled around him in the night as he slept outdoors could not penetrate the mountain hut. Inside its snug comfort Donald heard nothing, not even the snores of the young conscripts. He slipped easily into dreams of Ottoman sultans who coveted Kosovo's ravines, snow capped mountains, fertile plateaus, herds of wild horses in high pastures...

9

May 2, 1999

Donald awoke confused. Searching for clues in the gloom of unknown time and place, he traced back through his dreams to yesterday's end. The low hut was still murky, but today filled with sounds that gave it life. Plop...plop... the sound of dripping water brought relief that his hearing had returned. Hanging above him was a short shiny tube that suspended a single water drop. It fell into a bucket on the floor. A young Serb emptied the bucket into a pot on the primitive stove, a perforated oil drum raised on stones. Quick muttered Serbo-Croat exchanges came from bunks recessed along the walls. The falcon-eyed lad who rescued him yesterday sat on one of the rude bunks. His black ponytail tilted toward the upper bunk as he shaved over the basin Donald had washed in last night.

Serbo-Croat was a language Donald knew mainly through reading. Their conversation made no sense to him. But stiffly and slowly, he tried to speak to his rescuer. "Are you human or did I imagine you?"

"You imagined me. Hungry?" He put a cup and a

plate of fried potatoes and garlic with dried meat in front of Donald.

Expecting coffee, Donald lifted the cup to his lips. He was surprised to find two fingers of warm brandy instead. Coughing, he almost did not hear the Serb's question.

"Where does your imagination live?"

Donald translated carefully before answering, "In the sixteenth century. And you?"

"I'm trapped in the twelfth century."

"A twelfth century seer who appeared in the ravine when I fell yesterday?"

"Yes. I watch. Your bike went down the gorge, I'm afraid. Where are you going?"

"Looking for Kosovo's past. And you?"

"I'm watching for Kosovo's future. How will you get to Kosovo's past without your bike?"

"Will you direct me?"

"Can you walk down the mountain if I take you with me?"

Donald felt stiff from sleeping on a board and was eager to leave the gloomy room to walk by limestone gorges and racing rivers. Hoisting his pack on his back, he stepped out into a half-foot of new snow. A scrim of mist swathed the mountaintop, so all he saw was white.

"No jets this morning. This is not bombing weather. Still, you are safer walking except for the mines. You have to know where you walk." He slipped Donald's pack off and flipped it on his own shoulder.

Donald glanced quickly back to see only a dead tree fallen over a large boulder with no sign of the mountain hut. The moist unmoving air kept secrets and suspended fragrances in isolated outdoor rooms. Donald left the pocket of wood smoke and moved into a pine scented one. Pine needles dispensed melted snow, drop by drop. Nothing else moved. In silence he followed a trailless route down through a clammy succession of scents. Seeing only a few yards in any direction, tree branches and brambles seemed to leap out at him, fresh and damp in the half-light. As they descended, all trace of snow disappeared, replaced by slippery leaf mold and damp grasses that wet his ankles.

Turning round the sheer wall of a butte, the trail narrowed to a foot's width. On the far side they came out onto a small grassy plateau, precariously sloping down. The land fell away in front of his feet with no horizontal pause. Donald nudged a stone over the edge. Falling down the rocky wall, its echo multiplied as though dozens of stones were falling to the unseen below. A rock dove plunged after it. In front of them white spray hung suspended in the air. Within it a slender waterfall leapt from a great bare precipice and plummeted down, disappearing into the narrow gorge. His guide turned into the forest and hurried on.

For hours they walked, stopping only for gulps of

frigid water from the stream. Edged with thin ribbons of ice high in the mountain, it became gorged with melting snow as it fell, twisting in and out of sight in its headlong rush to the bottom. Even when the rapids disappeared in the densest parts of the forest, he could hear the stream racing ahead of him. 'Swift, swift' its whisper echoed through the forest.

When they reached a gentle slope of beech trees, the water quieted enough for him to hear chattering blackbirds. The drifting mist had retreated above the highest treetops and the copse around him was entirely visible. Beyond a bosky thicket, they stopped at a spring-fed pool as clear as glass. Donald squatted on a stone at its edge, but hesitated, not wanting to break the surface.

"See where it gurgles up? It invites you. 'Drink,' it says. No? 'Drink!'" The Serb urged and finished drinking.

Still Donald peered down into the pool's green and rocky blackness.

"Are you tired?"

"Only thinking of the bottom." Donald put his face close to the surface and lapped hesitantly with his tongue. The silken water tasted of sweet mountain air. It was of such purity, he felt he polluted it by drinking.

"It's not far to the bottom," his guide assured him.

Donald thought about going down into the iridescent greens that glowed in the underwater world. *Not far. Not far.*

"To the bottom of the mountain," he urged.

The thick black hair and camouflage shoulders disappeared into the trees.

Rising reluctantly from his knees, Donald stumbled after him over roots and stones. Gray withered spikes of Christ's thorn tore at his jacket. Rustling, snapping, crunching, he followed the lad who glided silently. The leaf canopy changed from pines to oaks, ash, aspen, and chestnut trees. The mist enveloped them so he had no sense of where he was.

Finally, they stopped again under a gnarly mulberry tree.

"Follow this stream. A kilometer on it will take you to a farmhouse. There you can spend the night. Tomorrow you can walk on to Prizren. Stay away from the roads. UCK mined them. You should return to the twentieth century. Kosovo is dangerous for everyone now." The lad spoke softly, as though in fear of being overheard. Yet they'd seen no one in the forest all morning. Donald's whole field trip had been solitary until he fell off his bicycle and was rescued.

Without understanding the reason for caution, Donald responded in a whisper.

"I'm sure you are right. Thank you for my visit to your mountaintop,"

"You won't tell anyone about it, will you?" He set the backpack on Donald's shoulder.

"The magic hut?" It was an odd request Donald

thought. "No, never. If I did, it would disappear."

"Yes. It would disappear." Making the Serbian sign of the trinity with his thumb and two fingers, he turned away and was swallowed by mist.

Donald was alone once more. *UCK mines? What did that mean?* The gurgling stream urged him along. Under a tree he noticed wild mushrooms and realized he was hungry. He left the stream to search for more mushrooms and gathered as many as he could until he reached another spring at the base of a sheer rock outcropping. Donald sat down gratefully in a soft bed of ferns. Along the edge of the pool was watercress. He picked handfuls, rinsed it in the water and ate it with the mushrooms. He leaned back against the soft velvety moss, avoiding trickles of water dripping down the rock face through brown and red lichen. His eyelids drooped. The mushroom and watercress flavors remained in his mouth. The soft dripping of water reminded him of waking this morning. That seemed so long ago. The hours of scurrying after his guide had tired him.

It was sometime later that he woke to muffled, undoubtedly cockney-accented conversation not far from his ear. It startled him so that he did not dare move, only cautiously opening his eyes. There was no one, yet he clearly heard, "That Serb courier on a bicycle you hit yesterday… one of his MUP contacts…he was in the uniform. He came running down the side of the mountain and got the body before we could get to it. Took his document pouch too."

It must have been a dream. But the labored breathing was too real. Donald's head was next to a wide crevice where he felt a breeze. He pressed his ear into it. There was only silence. Then the same voice spoke again. "We missed that intelligence. But he gave away their position. The MUP command post is on top of that mountain. I can't find the road up to it, but that was where the spy was headed. We need to hit it."

Donald turned his head slowly, searching everywhere around him, still no sign of anyone. The rock he leaned against rose straight up to an outcropping of trees forty feet above him. The silence was broken again and he quickly turned his ear back to the crevice to catch a few more words.

"Hit it tonight!"

Donald listened intently. *Serb couriers on bikes? How very strange. He hadn't seen any Serbs on bikes. It sounds like a phone call. How could someone be out here on a telephone? It's as though I suddenly wandered past the Waterloo Station public phone booths.*

"It's 500 meters at 4 o'clock from Lucy."

For a quarter of an hour, he sat waiting and listening for more about Lucy and Serb couriers. There was nothing more. Donald retraced his steps to the stream. He continued his journey refreshed and less hurried. The stream too was less hectic, snaking in loops through gentle inclines.

When the mountain was behind him, he was in a softer world. The stream stopped rushing and became sweet natured. Around his feet were cowslips and violets. A frightened hare took flight, hopping away from Donald across the dark furrows of a plowed field. Beyond it sheep nosed the ground, methodically gorging on new green sprouts.

Serb couriers on bicycles, Cockneys meeting Lucy in the forest, UCK mines and now a pastoral scene as placid as any he could imagine. Kosovo was a land of the unexpected.

10

May 2, 1999

The mist was pierced by a sad low song borne on an otherworldly tone. The narrow quartertones and fifth tones of the melodies fell between the scale familiar to Donald's ears. Following the irresistible music, he forgot his instructions. Beyond an orchard, a thread of smoke rose from the chimney of a house that settled comfortably into the land. The same stones that littered the stream emerged at the corners of the house and were laid in dry courses for the stable.

The singer looked as exotic as his music. Above a wavy white mustache, his large gray eyes shone with an inner vision of his tale. A short black vest hung loose below his white stand-up collar. Voluminous cuffless shirtsleeves flowed like wings from his large frame. An unrecognizable instrument rested between the knees of his worn britches. Slowly he drew the bow across, and even more slowly back, to yield a plaintive sound that expressed this wild land. It seemed to live and breathe, to stretch to a high note and almost run out before the end of the phrase. Soon the dark-toned voice followed along the same path. Bow and voice came together and parted again, each leading, then accompanying by turn.

Donald crept past the stable, wanting to hear every word.

The music stopped and the singer called out, "God bless you!"

Donald hesitated, then answered, "Health and peace to you."

"Sit down, Traveler, you must be thirsty and tired." He nodded toward a bench next to a handmade pitchfork offering a three-fingered salute.

With more confidence Donald repeated the old-fashioned Serbian greeting when a woman came out the door carrying a tray of tea for two. Watching and imitating Petar, Donald tasted the preserves, then water, followed by tea. The ballad continued to vibrate through him. *Fog fell upon the Bojana.*

Birds frantic at the coming night flapped back and forth between the trees. In a final triumph, banishing all mist at the end of the day, the mountain shimmered in a glow of light. A flight of bats swirled up against the sky. Just as suddenly the sun was extinguished. The darkness felt deeper after the unexpected bloom of sunset. Field mice left their burrows. The first owl hooted across the valley. Nighthawks called. Leposava lit a lantern and bustled them indoors.

The household was a remnant from the past. Haunted by song, every creak and groan of the floors, rafters and hinges seemed musical. On the stove a pot bubbled beside frying potatoes and onions, filling the room with rich meaty smells. The simple wooden table, chairs and vessels showed traces of the tools that had shaped them. Petar gave Donald the best seat on the opposite side of the stove from the door. Over supper of spicy bean soup with chunks of dried meat, Donald felt he was almost expected—the stranger in old Serbian tales who arrives one day and stays.

"It smells of rain." Petar broke into Donald's medieval fantasy.

"The water barrels are full. You better have a bath," Leposava urged Donald. "The rain will fill them up again tonight."

She lifted the copper boiler onto the stove. Donald brought in buckets of water from the stream to fill it. Petar turned up the round wooden ottoman and took it outdoors, setting it under a rain barrel. After supper, when the water reached a boil, Petar and Donald each took one handle of the copper pot and carried it outdoors. Balancing it on edge, they tipped boiling water into the wooden tub. Petar showed Donald how to open the plug to add cold water from the rain barrel until the temperature was right.

Donald picked up the pail and half filled it with water from the tub. Taking off his shoes and socks, he put one foot then the other in the pail. He removed the rest of his clothes and poured the water over himself. After soaping, he refilled the pail and stepped back into it to remove the soap from his feet before tipping it over his head and body. Only then did he get into the tub. Instantly, every muscle melted in the heat. Limp with contentment, he could have stayed in the soothing hot bath for hours. Around him all was dark except the glow-worms floating above the meadow. From the fields, a breeze brought damp odors of new green shoots. There were night noises from the animals, the woods, and more thunder in the sky. From high above him the howl of a wolf rolled down the mountain. Donald leaned back his head and looked up into the night sky. A dazzling streak of light exploded on top of the mountain. The mountaintop glowed daylight bright in a bonfire as big as the hut where he had slept last night. A choir of tree boughs shrieked and gave off a funereal moan as a gust of wind caught and held them. More thunder reminded him to get out of the bath so Leposava and Petar could have their turns before the rain. The fresh cold air blew across his wet body as he rubbed himself with a linen towel. Shivering, he threw on his shirt and pants and returned to the warm glow of the kitchen.

In the sitting room they showed him a narrow wooden bed, with head and footboards of the same low height. Along the wall embroidered pillows made it fancy seating when not serving as a bed. Under the black diamond-patterned blanket were hand woven linen sheets and a goose down pillow made by Leposava. Donald slid gratefully into the sleepy pleasure of a bed indoors.

11

Donald fell effortlessly into the rhythm of the farm. Each morning he opened his eyes on the opanci casting a sundial shadow on the wall. Another day of sampling new skills and tastes began. He tried milking the cow. He shelled corn from the corncrib for the chickens. He hoed Leposava's vegetable garden. Under the spell of their valley, he was glad to let the world beyond it float away. To him their farm lives were irresistibly exotic. Though reluctant to pry, he longed to know their histories. One chilly evening Petar told his tale.

"My father Cedomir Cajkanovic could follow the scent of a hare. From him I learned to trap rabbits. My mother was Zagorka Illic. After she milked the cow, she cooked milk in the kettle. I would sit on a low stool and wait to drink it for my supper. I still remember the taste of milk in that wooden bowl.

"We fasted on Wednesdays and Fridays, not just on Christmas Eve. On Easter Sunday we had a glass of wine. If we went to market day, we carried white bread with us so people would not know we were poor. Going to market and eating white bread, too—ah, what could be better? Once my uncle bought me a pair of opanci in Prizren for our Slava-Petkovdan, October 27."

St. Petka's day, Donald translated to himself.

"They hang beside your bed," Leposava whispered to Donald as she absently kneaded bread for tomorrow.

"Every evening before going off to bed we stood with our lighted candles and bowed our heads. We crossed ourselves and prayed for peace, health, the animals and the harvest. We asked the saints to bless our home."

Donald barely caught sight of Leposava swiftly crossing herself before her hand disappeared again into the dough. Rising plumply between her fingers, its yeasty fragrance blossomed in the kitchen.

"I was born in a village fifteen kilometers away. In my fifth year I went to live in my grandfather's house with my uncle's family. Grandfather was rich because he was the only child of parents who had worked hard and been wise in everything they did. His trousers were ornamented with braid and his sash was fat with money from selling pigs and wine, wood and hens. He became staresina early because he was so much trouble to his parents. All of us in the zadruga did what would please him. When he pulled out his long ebony pipe with the amber mouthpiece, his daughters-in-law and the wives of his cousins ran to get a coal and his tobacco pouch. When he wanted something else, he would cough. We offered him anything he might want. Nodding or tapping his heels impatiently, he waved away what we offered. So ashamed was he at his uneducated speech that he would not talk for days at a time though he had two fine gold teeth to show off.

"Old people in the village whispered that he was lazy and bad from childhood and did not go to school most of the time. He stayed illiterate all his life. His two sons did go to school as their grandparents wished. Father was sometimes lazy, although he was not a bad man. He danced well and was a good singer. You could say less for a dozen men.

"Grandfather had many other peasants working for him because he had inherited so much land and because he was lazy. He was bad to them and bad to their wives but they needed the jobs. Behind his back they took what they wanted. I saw peasants slyly steal eggs, chickens or wheat. Sometimes even a piglet. I did not tell because they were so mistreated. Grandfather would be drunk and not notice and never did he keep count of what he owned.

"Because of his debts, he started losing the land. After supper while Grandfather snored over his rakija, the other men in the family sat up late, worrying for our future. They cut tobacco from their pouches, rubbed it, filled their pipes. The smoke curled out of their mouths and filled the ceiling. All night they were shaking their heads about the ruin our staresina was bringing. By morning their pouches were flat and the room was hazy with smoke. Grandfather was in no mood to listen to good advice the next day or the next week, not even after the last remnant of the zadruga broke up."

The bellowing of an ox startled Donald and ended Petar's tale.

Setting her dough to rise at the back of the stove, Leposava wrapped herself in a large shawl and sat down on her three-legged chair. "We haven't had a song tonight."

Petar curled each side of his mustache round his finger, drank the last of his rakija, then picked up his gusle. The single string blended with his singing, spinning out a long fluid musical line. Centuries flowed through Petar, the music playing him.

12

For some nights after Donald arrived at the farm, distant thunder brought no rain. When finally, black storm clouds hung low, blotting out the sky and mountains, there was no thunder and the animals were peaceful. Ahead of the rain, Petar hurried the bleating sheep, not even pulling burrs from their legs until they were back in the pen. A sudden warm splash of drops drove up the smell of earth. Donald inhaled deeply, savoring it before he went in for supper.

The rain brought an early evening and a quiet night with no thunder. Donald slept deeply to the rustling of maple boughs. At dawn, it was still raining and blowing. Tree branches tossed and rolled, scattering leaves through the air. The blurry green aquarium outside his window sent him back into peaceful dreams until the rain stopped.

Long after he heard the hollow clanging of sheep bells as Petar drove them to pasture, Donald finally appeared, very hungry, in the kitchen. Berkeley cappuccino bars opened at this late hour, but farmers like Petar and Leposava had been working half their day. The basin of warm water had gone cold waiting for him. He washed, then made himself a large breakfast of tea, jam and fresh eggs with Leposava's cornmeal cakes. In Berkeley he never ate like this. By the time he got to work outdoors, it was near their dinnertime. Sheepishly, he helped gather the first edible greens. A snail fell from a reluctant stalk as he pulled it out. Leposava told him it would be easy to collect them after the rain. Intent on gathering a large serving of snails, Donald methodically worked his way through the damp garden to the edge of the field.

Fog swallowed the mountains and crept into the valley. The oxen were indistinct frescos on the white fog wall. Coaxed by Petar's singsong chant, they strained forward under a high yoke hitched to the plow. Petar leaned into it, one hand on each end of the wide wooden V. Expertly balancing the plow and guiding the team with the leather strap wound round his waist and shoulders, he turned up fresh loam in furrows straight and deep for sowing. End to end across the field Bela and Boris plodded, gathering clods of mud that weighed down their legs. It clung thicker and thicker, slowing their movement. When Petar unyoked the oxen and came in for the evening, his knee-high boots were coated in mud like the oxen's legs. The layered calluses on his hands were rubbed red and raw. "Our month of rain gave the field a good soaking,"

"Rain is the weeping of angels. This spring had too many tears. Better to rely on melting snow than angel's tears,"

Leposava said.

"It's the absence of rain that makes a farmer cry. We are eager to lose the snow, my wheat and I." Petar looked at his wife with bemused appreciation. "My snow rabbit loves it. When the fields turn brown and winter retreats higher up the mountain each day, the snowshoe rabbits are reminders it leaves behind. They hop out of the forest after sunset, moonlight catching their white coats shining against the brown earth. They are the only white left in the spring world. Not for long—they give up their white coats when snow leaves their burrow. Their fur turns brown and they disappear once more." Petar leaned toward Donald to tell his secret. "If you want to know where their burrow is, watch when they turn brown.

"One year there were too many rabbits. I had to trap them or they would eat up the garden. Each day I marked the snowline with a stick where I found their paw prints. When they turned brown, I stopped looking for prints in the snow and found their burrow between the sticks. My traps were not empty as long as I put them out."

"We had rabbits hanging from the rafters and rabbit stew every dinner," Leposava rolled her eyes at the memory.

Donald could imagine them hanging above the kitchen. "Maybe I could catch a rabbit for dinner? Rabbit stew!" Excited by the idea, he asked Petar to show him how to set traps. It was not many days before he had a rabbit. And another and another. Though Petar and Leposava wanted the rabbits kept out of the garden and welcomed the provisions, Donald grew tired of daily rabbit stew. When the morning was clear, he went to the stream to fish instead of setting traps.

A flat boulder that parted the stream dried in the morning sun to make a seat for fishing. The current swished and swirled around it with a docile murmur. Far above in the black mountain, the frothing water tumbled over rocks in rushing falls. Beside the field long irrigation channels drank the highest water. Downstream where the oxen and cow went to drink, the water was quiet between smooth green banks. Its glassy surface mirrored the row of poplars, their leaves flashing silver in every breeze. Beyond the house, the stream meandered through the meadow to the forest.

Waiting for a nibble on his line, Donald came to know the small world of the stream. Even when he sat motionless, his shadow undulated with the ripples. Wherever it fell, trout shot quickly away. He could look down through a twisted knot of submerged branches to the bottom where small fish darted in and out of rocks, indifferent to his moving shadow. The delicate tracery of a spider's web fell across the surface until a breeze blew it apart. A beetle caught in its glistening threads leapt desperately to freedom, only to flop into the water, a surprising treat for a brown trout. A cricket tipped off a blade of grass, plunging after the beetle into the stream. Hatching mayflies took flight, luring fish to the surface. Lizards rustled through the grass. Young frogs were awkward acrobats, jumping in and out of the stream. A grouse landed on a rock, flicked his tail and drank from the stream. Retreating to the stone wall he inflated his red throat sack, spun and fanned his tail in a mad mating dance. He was hustled offstage by the strange loud clacking of a Balkan turkey grouse. Glowering under prominent red eyebrows, he belligerently paced his ramparts. Even a bird as large as he could not patrol walls that rambled through garden, orchard and field. Stones cleared for the sake of a plow had metamorphosed into manmade imitations of the mountains that walled in the quiet valley.

More than protective walls, the mountains were capricious comrades, altering throughout the day. When the noon sun was bright, their high ridgelines were sharply etched against the sky. When clouds were heavy or the mists clung thickly to them, they became blue phantoms. The mountains' shifting shades beguiled Donald. In the first rosy light their folds disappeared into blackened shadow. Throughout the day color shifted from gray, green, brown, through gold before the peaks turned to rust in the last blaze of the sinking sun. In the minutes after sunset they were purple. Whether Donald was fishing, hoeing the garden or setting rabbit traps, he'd look up and be surprised at the color. *When did they change? I didn't see it happen.* Another day had ended so quickly.

After supper Petar would take up his long flat-bellied gusle. Each night he sang a different song. "The old blind woman who taught me knew a thousand if she knew her name."

Donald could only shake his head in amazement. "How do you remember those epic poems? They are so long."

"Remembering is the Serbian necessity. We look back on giants and know that we are humble, not heroes. Byzantine border guards sang their adventures to gain courage for new attacks morning could bring. Longing for the vines they planted, the wife they married short days before duty, they praised the horse that carried them safely back from death for another day. Slav peasants took up the songs and told their own battles of life and love."

"How do you choose which to sing?"

"I'm always waiting for my next song. The tale that needs telling comes. I find myself in it and follow."

Petar stroked the hairy string until it moaned like a sad wind. Slowly he began telling the fall of Bosna. After siege and desperate battle the Turks triumphed, bringing devastation, prison and painful loss.

"my Syrian apple and my sweet little child

they also took Bogdanos' son"

The chant carried Donald back a millennium to the eastern reaches of the Byzantine Empire. Night images borne on the wailing string blended into dreams.

13

In the middle of the night the windows rattled violently and the house shuddered.

For once the thunder did not stop with first light. The house was nervous. Every roll of thunder set the sheep bleating, the cow lowing and made the oxen shift towards the stable.

After breakfast Leposava stood in the yard looking up. "What a strange spring we're having. What's the matter with the sky?" Then she shook her head and took the fresh milk into the kitchen. "Did the thunder wake you?" She asked Donald as he ate his breakfast.

"Yes." The strange rattling had disturbed his dreams until morning.

"A bad night!"

Donald went to the open door. "No rain? There's only dew on the grass."

"No, no rain, only dry thunder. Grandfather warned of war's dry thunder." She looked out the window toward the maple tree, remembering his reappearance. When she was three years old a living scarecrow limped across the meadow in slow motion. On a handmade crutch and one leg, her half-starved grandfather dragged himself to the maple tree. The boot on his foot was in shreds. Around his shoulders was the blanket that had been his coat as he walked in the cold and his bed at night. He seemed to stand there for hours. Even now, that was how she remembered him. Today she seemed to expect to see him there. "You read Serbo-Croat?"

Donald washed his breakfast plate. "Better than I speak, I hope."

"My eyes are not what they were." Leposava set a stained and ragged schoolboy's notebook on the table in front of Donald.

"He came home from the war weakened by a diet of scant grains from ravaged farms and thorns from the wintry forests. He barely had strength to die at home."

As he would for the fragile old manuscripts he studied, Donald gently lifted a page with only a fingertip. Leposava closed her eyes as he began reading to her.

"November 25—" Donald squinted at the cramped writing.

"The fall brought muddy roads and oats for the horses became scarce. It gets worse as winter comes. There was great difficulty shoeing two horses tonight. We have no more winter horseshoes. It feels like snow will be in our faces tomorrow and under the poor shoes of men and beasts. Horses are falling over from lack of feed. They lie beside the road, dying. Men fall with them, exhausted, faint from hunger, frostbitten by bitter cold. Our bivouacs are no more than a bit of straw to lie on. No field kitchens, no bread most of the month. The men fall asleep in their sad quarters with little of an evening meal. The slender rations only augmented if fowl are shot and cooked. Some men gave up their sleep to bake rough bread for us to have today.

"The horses stood out all night in the wind beside this drafty barn overflowing with men. The night was dark, unlit by stars. I could not write until this dawn. Once again came the brave patrol and his horse bringing more bad news of the Bulgarian advance, their numbers, and the hardship to the Serbian people they drive out as they advance on Metohija."

Leposava remained immobile, standing over him.

Perhaps she is impatient, wanting to get back outdoors to her chores? Donald handed the journal back to her. She thanked him and held it, rubbing it gently with her thumb. Still she did not move.

"Let me feed the chickens today. You showed me how. I think I can do it."

Leposava said nothing in reply. Sinking into a chair, she nodded slightly.

In the yard Donald tried to imitate Leposava's call, "Kvok, Kvok, Kvok!" He tried clucking. At last the rattle of the corn bucket brought a dozen hens fluttering around Donald's feet. They fell on the grain with enthusiasm as soon as it hit the ground. The feeding was going well until the cock approached. His wings were low and his ruff rose around his head. Ignoring the corn, he pecked at Donald's calves. Donald yelped in surprise and then annoyance as the cock continued his assault. Dropping the bucket, he ran, pursued by the triumphant cock.

Leposava did not appear in the garden the rest of the morning. Donald kept busy—pulling up nettles, weeding the spring lettuce and cabbage, and digging up a cluster of potatoes hidden under sinewy mounds

In the afternoon he followed Leposava through the orchard. Blossoms opened too easily in the belated sun, spreading their intense bouquets under the canopy of branches. The sun fell through the sieve of leaves onto small violet flowers.

"That cat's foot is for gout or sore throat. The adder's tongue for burns or sore eyes."

She showed him the carpet of blue sicklewort, white anemone, red nettles, bilberries, and pink snakeweed. Each had its uses. "The cures only work if they are mixed for the person who is ill in exactly the right quantity." Early in the spring she gathered her herbs with a hint of frost still on them before they flowered and lost their flavor. She revealed the extravagant abundance where his careless footfalls and idle thoughts had left them hidden. This time he saw it all through her intimate knowledge.

"You have kept yourself and Petar well with this wisdom."

"Except once." Leposava looked back beyond the house. "I avoided bad omens during my pregnancy. When mother died, I wore the red string around my wrist to protect the baby from the funeral. My labor started and babica delivered him before midnight the same evening. A healthy baby grew to be a strong little boy. There was no reason for him to die." Her voice trembled and her gray eyes were watery. "Nema veze," Never mind, she whispered, as she turned away.

Donald scolded himself for his curiosity or discomfort or both. First her grandfather's journal and now this! The shadows in her history haunted the silence.

A grasshopper jumped out of the grass across his shoe. It was a chance to step away from his frozen discomfort. He stepped on wild mint. It crushed and exploded with scent. He stooped to pluck a handful, inhaling the fragrance. Leposava bent down, uncovering four twigs with a bit of fur stuck to it under the mint.

"A nest!" Donald exclaimed, relieved.

The graceful boughs of a brook willow trembled in a faint mountain breeze. They set off again towards the stream. Blackbirds flew up out of the grass ahead of them. She knew the flights of birds that foretold a storm and could imitate their calls on the small flute Petar had carved for her.

Downstream she pointed to red butterbur. Near the yard was a yellow flowered celandine. "The last one I'll see this spring." Beneath the blue bells of wild hyacinth were violet flowers of creeping periwinkle.

"Were they all really here the day I came?"

In the garden carrots slipped out of the dark earth easily when Donald tugged what Leposava chose.

The mountains darkened and drew closer, swallowing the farm in evening. Fire sputtered in the stove under the soup. Leposava lit wicks in the lamps. Tonight Petar sang ten syllable lines of a tragic ballad. It fit the day's strange distress. The heavy horsehair string came to life like a snake under Petar's bow. His fingers had been motionless. Now they scurried with masterful delicacy along the gusle's neck, filling the room with sad thoughts. Outside, the wind howled around the corner of the house, then subsided as suddenly as it had begun. Calm descended on the farm with Petar's song.

When it ended, Leposava left the kitchen without a word. Petar set down the gusle and took up a candle to follow his wife to bed. "The Serbs have too much history," Petar said as he closed their door.

Donald sat transfixed, not moving from his chair in the kitchen. He could not tear his mind away from the power of the story and the music.

From behind the bedroom door came the easy rhythm of Petar's snoring whistles.

14

June, 1999

The trap was empty and the fish didn't bite. For dinner without rabbit or fish, Petar slaughtered a chicken or lamb. A month spent too freely on the stranger left the cold cellar bare and the flocks depleted. Donald's visit had to end.

At the edge of the orchard Donald lay on long grass that bent softly beneath him. Before tomorrow's departure, he wanted to record this life in the hem of the Cruel Mountains. Sunlight shimmered through leaves onto a blank page. Words didn't come. How could he capture the power of homely creations— the pitchfork, washboard, barrel, loom—that sustained Petar and Leposava? His head drooped low over his notebook. The pen slipped from his hand. Even bees were languid in the heat of the slow summery afternoon.

Two white Ural owls calling to each other across the yard woke him from his nap. The first evening wind brought heady scents of onions, garlic and paprika from bean soup.

After supper, the evening held onto the warmth of the day. Petar was on the stump with his gusle but he made no move to play it.

Donald found himself struggling with his Serbo-Croat for gratitude. It was easiest to revert to Petar's music. "I had never heard a gusle."

Petar looked surprised, "You don't have maple trees?"

"Yes, many. But no gusles."

Petar nodded toward the old maple standing outside Donald's window. "A branch fell one night. She worried it was a bad omen for our marriage. But it was a gift welcoming me to Leposava's house. The gift of music to play for her." Not taking his eyes off Leposava, he picked up his gusle and bow and began searching for a tune. He was in a playful mood. There was laughter in the wandering sounds tonight.

Leposava started swaying and humming. Her arms shimmied up. Petar's random notes found their way into a dance tune.

"Show Donyald the Kolo!" Petar encouraged her.

Leposava took off her worn shoes and slung them over her shoulder. "Come!" she urged. Her movements were lithe and youthful. Donald struggled to his feet. She stretched one arm out straight from her shoulder and took hold of Donald's upper arm. He mimicked her as she kicked and stomped the ground. She moved around a half-circle. They bowed, joined hands at arm's length and turned, circling back. Then side-by-side they danced, knocking shoulders, clasping arms. Each move coincided with the lively bowing of the gusle. Rocking her white head gaily, she shot her husband a glance. He beamed at his frisky wife and began blunt plucking a sound of galloping horses. The house and stable spun past as wild horses pounded on. Leposava's elbows and knees flew in and out as her bare feet slapped the grass. Faster and faster they whirled until the mountains blurred into a circle around them. The gusle's strange string didn't relent under Petar's fast bowing.

Donald fell down in a dizzy twirl. Above him leaves shivered in the breeze of Leposava's dance. Tired at last, she sank to the grass, laughing until tears came to her eyes. Shaking with laughter and wiping away tears, she stuffed a piece of honey cake in her mouth. Her cheeks ballooned out in two round pouches. Escaping crumbs drifted over her sleeves and apron and sprinkled the grass.

Honey cake sweetened Donald's mouth. Tender perfume from old roses blew over him. Two birds hovered lazily above Petar, as though in the tree his stump had been. Tattered white puffs of cloud above them seemed to smile down on the heavy green evening. Donald closed his eyes, holding the memory of this moment, this valley and the dear people who took in a stranger so willingly.

At sunup next morning Donald walked away from the solitary farm. For the first and only time, he walked out of the front gate, crossing the boundary of their world. The leaves and grasses rustled under his feet. The sun warmed him. The meadow released its fragrances as he passed. It was a beautiful country.

At first he looked back every hundred yards. The house pulled back behind its wall and sank into the undulating meadow. Then he glanced back and saw no house. How could that happen? He stopped and looked more intently, trying to see a bit of the roof. A glimpse of the chimney surely! The wind sighed and the grasses trembled. Darting swallows shrieked despairingly above him. Despite the hot Balkan sun, Donald shivered.

The enigmatic Serb may not be of this world, dematerializing when you turn away. The mountain sprite evaporated into fog. Leposava's house disappeared with nothing more than meadow grass to hide it. *Was I really there? I couldn't invent Petar's music.* In the pack on his shoulder a jar of honey, wooden flask of rakija, cheese and cornmeal cake were bulky realities prepared for his journey. A guest must not leave empty-handed, Leposava insisted. They are real. He wanted to retrace his steps to see the stone farmhouse once more. But there was only meadow grass, tall and golden all the way to the Cruel Mountains. Resigning himself, he turned away, setting his course toward Prizren and Bayram.

15

Bogdan stood silently beside Petar's stump, unseen. It was as though he had just unloaded wood for them.

Petar noticed him first and walked over from the stable. "We're glad you came back for a visit."

Leposava came out the kitchen door holding a glass toward him. "You didn't even have a rakija last time."

The first drop he spilled on the ground, giving it back to the earth before he drank. "Good health!" he saluted them both.

"Sit down," Leposava urged him, pointing to the bench beside her.

Leaning back against their house, Bogdan drank again. He stared off past the wooden beehive, toward the end of the thirty hectare farm and beyond, to the craggy mountains. The narrow valley was peaceful in the summer morning. It seemed to refute the purpose of his visit this morning when he should be racing to the Kosovo border. *I don't know what to say. Should I tell them to pack up and leave, while they are still alive? The Italians might not take care of them.*

Instead he quietly told them. "I came to say goodbye. The Italians are taking over here." *It's Besnik Citaku who'll really be in charge. Citaku boys chopped off the fingers of the best army sniper we ever had here.*

"They're coming back?" Leposava shifted on the bench in surprise.

Bogdan was startled. "You had Italian visitors already?"

"No. The Italians took over before. In the war." Petar explained.

"Oh!" *They're talking about Mussolini.* "Well, I don't want you to be kidnapped again because I won't be here. All Serb police must leave."

"The Italians are running things again?"

"Yes. They're the ones to protect you now." *They have survived so much. Perhaps they still can.* He wanted to convince himself.

"They didn't protect Djordje last time," Leposava said

"Djordje?"

"What did it accomplish to shoot that sentry? It only made the Germans mad and they killed the children." Petar could not forget the pointless attack.

"I know," Bogdan said, though he hadn't been born yet. He'd heard of the children murdered by Nazis. *So their child was one of them? Nasty! Good thing it's Germans in Prizren, not Pec and Djakovica.* "No more Serb police to worry about you. If you have a problem, you have to go to KFOR."

"We never have a problem," Petar insisted.

"In March you had a problem," Bogdan reminded them.

"You took care of that," Leposava nodded appreciatively.

"We've been busy since then. The winter wheat to bring in. Bela and Boris threshed it." Petar jerked his head toward a stake in the middle of a matted circle of grass.

Bogdan had been too preoccupied to notice. Now he saw the scattered tan grains and stems. He pulled out a fat husk tangled in the grass near his shoe and crushed it, slowly inhaling its sunny piquancy. *I've never seen threshing that old way!*

"The falcon will fly back to his mountain. The valley will not be the same. We're too busy to worry about that," Petar added.

"I do," Bogdan said under his breath, scattering the chaff fragments on the grass in a sowing motion. "Is there anything I can do before I leave?"

"Oh, we're fine here, like always," Petar assured him.

Flies circled endlessly above, each buzz briefly going from high to low in alternating choruses. Bogdan watched them aimlessly as he thought about what this old couple was saying. They hadn't mentioned the war. *All the bomb attacks since their kidnapping, and they heard none of them?* "You don't get electricity out here. I suppose you haven't been listening to the radio?"

"No, never had one—makes a racket."

"You're way out of the way. Maybe no one will come here to bother you."

"We had a visitor," Leposava said.

"What do you mean?" Bogdan was sure it was an Albanian. Maybe the war did come to them.

"A foreigner came through here and stayed with us."

"A foreigner? What kind of foreigner?"

"An American."

Bogdan sat forward, startled. "American? What was an American doing here? How did he get here?"

"He walked right to the house. Came along the stream."

Bogdan looked at the stream and followed it out of sight. "He came from that mountain? Where the stream comes from?"

"Yes. He came down out of the Cruel Mountains."

"How did he get past the Ottoman bridge at Djakovica? We had a checkpoint there."

"I don't know that he was ever in Djakovica."

"When did he come? The night I brought you back?" Bogdan had worried afterwards that his tracks in the snow or the lights from his Niva might have given away their small hidden valley.

"Oh, no, long after that. After you brought us home, the rain poured out of the sky until the end of April. The stream was a torrent driving rocks and tree branches past the field." Petar sat down on the stump, eager to talk of mud. "The meadow you drove across became a sea of mud, cutting us off from the road until after the rain stopped. Mud so thick, it fights to hold your foot down in it with each step. If you stand still, it feels that you cannot lift either leg and you will die right there, trapped in it. It takes practice to get through it without losing a boot. The mud leaves a crust on the boots. Better not to scrape off. Leave them to dry in the sun or behind a stove and knock the mud off. If you scrape off the crust while its damp to go on working, it doesn't all come. But the dead weight will become immobile if you don't."

"We were deep in mud. To keep out of the house—it's a job!" Leposava wholeheartedly agreed.

Bogdan drank again from his rakija. He wasn't interested in mud. Every moment he delayed here increased the peril of the road out of Kosovo but he could not rush them. "How long was he here?"

"For weeks," Leposava considered. "Maybe a month."

"For weeks? A month! An American was here this spring for a month and the police never heard about it?"

"We've seen no one but you since he left. We didn't

tell anyone he was here. I don't know who he told."

"He was a spy? He had a gun and a laser?"

"Oh, no gun. He arrived with nothing."

"What kind of soldier was he?"

"He wasn't a soldier at all. He was so thin. When I saw him walking towards the house, coming down the stream out of the mountains, it was like when my grandfather came home so thin. Grandmother thought he had died defending Skopje, but he came back from the dead when the war was long over. Looking out my window that day, for a moment I thought it was someone come back from the dead." Then she whispered, "I thought it was my Djordje."

"How old was he?"

"He was nine. It was 1941."

"No. I'm sorry." Bogdan suppressed a groan and tried again to separate the recent event from their distant memories. "That is a terrible thing to live with. I meant how old was your visitor, the American?"

"He was older than he looked, but not like us."

"Well," Bogdan did not know how to get at this mystery. "What was he doing?"

"He gathered eggs and picked wild greens and mushrooms. He went fishing in the stream and caught nice fish."

"That's all?" Their answers were unsatisfactory.

"Oh, no. He trapped some rabbits for our dinner. He

liked Petar's songs."

"Where is he now? How long ago did he leave?"

"He left after breakfast. You might have met him on the road. He went to Prizren to get the bus to Macedonia. He's gong home on an airplane from Greece. Have you been on an airplane?"

"No, I'm pretty earthbound myself." Bogdan lifted his head against the fresh white lime plastered wall, looking up at the sky as though he expected to see the American's plane there.

"He finished the limewash yesterday and left this morning."

Bogdan pulled away from the wall suspiciously and sniffed at it. Finally he shook his head in puzzlement. "Why was he here? Why did he come?"

"We never asked. He was our guest."

"When did you say he came?"

"A month ago."

Bogdan leaned his chin on his left fist as he tried to work this out. "A month ago he came walking down that stream from the mountain. And beyond that mountain is a taller mountain that had a small army lookout post on top. It was a hawk's perch up there. A few conscripts manned it—watching for an invasion, watching for anything." As his eyes found the crest where the observation hut had been, a film of cloud swept across the shoulder of the mountain, leaving the peak to float between heaven and earth. "A month ago it was destroyed by a laser-guided bomb. All the boys were killed. Did he do that?"

The old couple knew nothing of lasers and hadn't seen any bombs.

Bogdan persisted, "What kind of communications equipment did he have—satellite phone, short-wave radio, that sort of thing?"

"We don't have a phone and we didn't see anything like that. He only had a small pack. Not even a bedroll."

"Did he go off on his own all day?"

"He never left the farm. The farthest he went was fishing under that tree." Petar began to look worried by all the strange questions about Donald.

"We didn't leave the farm after you brought us home and he didn't leave the farm until this morning," Leposava added. "He walked off as simply as he came."

Bogdan's wide face extended up to his receding hairline where his brown hair was tousled by the wind. The strains of this day, this month and this year had worn him out. It would be one last unsolved case to leave behind him in Kosovo. He'd try to work it out after he was safely in Nis. "I can't make anything of it," he said, downing the last gulp of rakija. *This strange case is someone else's worry now.*

"No, we've never had it happen before. People don't come visiting back here."

When he reached the road, Bogdan stopped the Niva to look south toward Prizren. *Should I go a kilometer or two to try to catch him? Then what?* Out of his right eye he caught movement from the Pec direction. A gang of Albanian boys startled him into bearing down on the gas. He tore out of the gap, spinning a cloud of dust, and turned north up the road. He had to hurry out of Kosovo before nightfall. It was easy to rationalize his decision. *That American has already done what he came to do. My police days here are over.*

16

return to Prizren June, 1999

Donald had been tramping up and down hills since breakfast. Left behind was the little valley where he spent a month too easily and quickly. The sun burned overhead as he zigzagged up a rocky slope of mauve thistles and asphodel. Reaching a small grassy tuft, he took off his shoes and wriggled his toes. On a flat rock beside him, he opened the carefully packed Serbian cheese and bread, cornmeal cake and honey. It was soon gone and the wooden flask held only a few more drops of rakija.

Lying down on the grass under an endless blue sky, he spotted an eagle floating high above him. He would like to return to Prizren as effortlessly as that eagle riding the wind. With a tremble of great wings, it curved into a circling pattern, then wheeled off beyond the highest peak. Losing sight of the bird, he scanned the face of inhospitable rock. In the shadows his eyes conceived suggestions of doors, crosses and even a church facade carved in the rock.

Blinking his eyes, he bolted upright. Was he peering into remnants of one of the ancient Serbian hermitages? The whiff of an earlier millennium excited him. Beside the stone hermitage a slender stream burst out of the rock and fell like a ribbon, vanishing into a defile. The road must be down there. He remembered the warning, *stay away from the road!* Yet it was tempting to see the hermitage, to prolong his stay in this unknown world that had enveloped him since he fell off his bicycle. *If it's real, how did anyone reach it?* There were no steps, nothing but sheer cliff below. Above it a shallow set of toeholds climbed up, then disappeared under a shady cache of snow at the peak where the eagle had flown. The climb to the hermitage looked difficult for anyone. Certainly, it was beyond him.

  Prizren was his imperative. Convinced of the climb's impossibility, he resumed his journey to Bayram. At the bottom of the rocky hill was a stream, narrow enough to cross in two leaps using a handy flat rock in the middle. On the far side a wooded slope loomed before him. He entered it and began to climb quite steeply, pushing through brambles and undergrowth. His backpack grew heavier and his weary legs ached. After several more hills and streams, he nearly gave in to the temptation of the road he had been warned to avoid. Instead, he rested on the rotting trunk of a fallen tree.

  Pushing on, he found himself on a mule path. At last he knew where he was! Every turn and tree was like an old friend. Around the next hill, the large valley of the Ottoman city opened up before him.

Near the first houses on the outskirts someone called out in Serbo-Croat, asking him the time. Looking around in confusion, he only saw an Albanian with an assault rifle facing him fifty meters down the road. *Why would he speak to me in Serbo-Croat?* That never happened before in Kosovo. After a long hesitation, he looked down at his watch and decided to answer in Albanian. "Dy pa nji çere."

Not caring about the time, the Albanian waved him on, revealing his own wristwatch. The Serbo-Croat question was repeated at every crossroad by groups of Albanians toting AK-47s. Chinese grenades nonchalantly banged against each other on their vests. Twice they asked for his ID. When he showed his American passport, they seemed to assume that, old as he was, he was an Albanian-American returning to join UCK. At least he was back in Prizren.

Bayram's house was near. Soon he'd nap on his divan. Over raki and Zeynep's tasty cooking he'd tell his friend all he'd seen.

17

The tsunami of Albanian enthusiasm surged over the city. Prizren had changed nationalities in his absence. Nowhere was there a Yugoslav flag, but the triumphant flag of Albania flamed everywhere. Even on Serb houses the black two-headed eagles left crimson bruises. Cyrillic signs were obliterated by paper substitutes or haphazard paint. Cheap echoey boom boxes blared from doorways, each playing the same Albanian song of liberation. "The day has come to defend our land! U-C-K! U-C-K!" It overlapped in an uncoordinated chorus down the street. Some new power had commandeered the city, supplying the flags and music.

Cloistered though he had been within Bayram's walls until the rains let up, Donald noticed alterations. When he set off on his bicycle five weeks earlier, it was cool and damp, just beginning to dry out from the month of rainfall. Now the sun scorched every surface and the river was quiet and low between the walls.

As he neared the Turkish district, rangy Albanians, armed to the teeth multiplied on every corner. Their kaleidoscope of camouflage fatigues were unified by the UCK patches sported on shoulders or black berets. *Where did they all come from?* With them, a few non-Albanians with long scrawny beards in bloused pants stared out into nothingness. They did not speak or look at him. More gun-toting Albanians rode in the backs of trucks roaring into town on the Albania road. Oversized fatigues hung loosely on their skinny frames.

At the Cafe Oaza his tired legs dropped gratefully onto an empty chair at the same table where he spent his last evening in Prizren. It still had the best view of the passing scene on both sides of the river. Recognizing the Albanian waiters smoking together at the edge of the cafe, he felt reassured.

His waiter smiled as though he remembered him and came over to take his order. Donald squinted at the back room where the Serb owner played cards with his Turkish friends. "Where is the owner today?"

The waiter's friendliness evaporated. Nervously wiping the table over and over with his soiled cloth, he looked away and mumbled, "Disappeared," before slinking off to the bar.

Disappeared, Donald thought. *How odd. Where are the Turks who played cards with him? Where are the gypsies?* They were simply gone. Today there were only Albanians.

A German tank followed by two armored trucks

and another Leopard tank rumbled down the street. Each was freshly painted with large white letters, "KFOR." Several Albanians on the sidewalks greeted them with calls of "Heil, Hitler!" The Germans flinched without responding.

Donald eagerly waited for his Turkish coffee. It had been more than a month since he'd had any.

A dozen heavily armed UCK fighters arrived, waving their weapons at the Albanian staff. Looking frightened, the waiters ran off down the street. The commander played a victory blast across the windows. As he threw his Chinese AK-47 back over his shoulder, the silver crescendo of falling shards of glass still echoed. One of the fighters jerked his head in Donald's direction and harshly whispered "cifut".

He is saying I'm a Jew, or a coward? Donald puzzled over which meaning was intended.

The young Albanian women at the table next to Donald's quickly slipped away. Still his coffee did not come. One of the UCK painted out the Cyrillic letters on the cafe sign.

Giving up on his coffee, Donald set off to Bayram's house. *No one makes better Turkish coffee than Zeynep.*

18

The gate would take him back to the serene life of the Ottoman house. The garden would be in its summer glory. After a nap on his divan, he was eager to see Bayram's translation of his manuscripts. Before flying back to Berkeley, he would have a week to explore Prizren.

Over the garden wall branches of lilac reached out to Donald, reassurance of tranquility. The strange disfiguration of Prizren could not reach Bayram's house. Thirsty and filled with eager anticipation, he pushed the gate open.

The alteration stunned him. It looked as though a blizzard had struck. Flower beds were out of sight beneath layers of Bayram's precious Siyakat documents. The centuries old parchments were bleaching and curling in the sun or submerged under water in the basin. Beneath the tree the broken quail's cage was empty. A parade of miniature Ottomans hung from the mandarin tree's branches like exotic fruits. The Humbaraci, dressed all in yellow, had a curving dagger in his wide striped cummerbund and black soutache edging his short vest over trousers that ballooned to the knee.

On his feet were flat red slippers like the ones Bayram wore. A bearded Timarli Sipahi wore a tall red turban with wide green vertical zigzags, red collarless jacket over a vest and blue trousers like Bayram's that reached to the tops of his red ankle boots. A pistol and small dagger were held in the fat gold coils of his cummerbund. A long rifle hung from his shoulder. Their broken frames and glass littered the gravel path.

Turning away from the distressing sight, Donald hurried to the house. One door was split, its metal cladding hanging loose. Frantically he turned the handle of the doorbell. "Bayram, Bayram!" he cried. He began pounding on the other door. It lurched in with a shrill screech across the tiles.

Three Albanian adolescents carelessly waving assault rifles confronted him.

For a long moment Donald said nothing. Then, wanting Bayram to hear him, he called out, "I'm a friend of Bayram's. He is expecting me."

"There is no Bayram here," someone answered.

Beyond the trio, Donald saw more Albanian boys. *Why are they here?* he wondered. *Who threw Bayram's papers into the garden?* He knew he could not ask these boys. "Where is Bayram?" was all he said.

"Byteqi!" they called.

A sweet-faced teenager came out of Bayram's salon. Across his narrow chest grenades were strung like a giant pineapple necklace. Tightly gripped in his hand was the

104

longest rifle Donald had ever seen, nothing like the assault weapons the others carried.

Is he really in charge? Donald was dubious. Uncomfortable with the relentless, unfriendly stares, he looked down and noticed a black ski mask hood hanging out of the boy's pocket. Bayram's embroidered slippers were on Byteqi's feet. Behind him was a pile of flags, large firecrackers and guns with the double-headed eagle and 'UCK' embossed on their wooden stocks.

"There is no Bayram," Byteqi repeated.

"This is Bayram's house," Donald said, more to confirm it to himself than convince them.

There was another long silence. Byteqi leaned over and whispered to a child. The little boy pushed past Donald and ran out the gate.

One of the older teens wearing a combined camouflage and black uniform held out a paper for Donald to read. It was a statement transferring ownership of the house to Byteqi Citaku. At the bottom was a signature so shaky it was hard to make out the name Bayram Zonguldak.

This could not be. How could Bayram give this boy his family house?

A firm hand gripped his shoulder. He looked into the barrel of a pistol. Above it, the unblinking eyes of the UCK soldier he had passed at the corner below Bayram's house.

Donald tried again. "I'm staying with my friend

Bayram."

The grip tightened. The soldier's eyes narrowed to slits of casual disdain. "The owner wants you to leave," he growled.

Donald apologized humbly, adding, "I'd just like to pick up my things from my room before I leave."

"The Turk's a thief!" one boy shouted and the others jeered in agreement.

With that, the soldier twisted Donald's arms together and stuck the barrel of the pistol in the hollow of his neck. The little boy forced a rigid plastic cuff on his wrists.

"Get moving." The soldier propelled him out the gate.

Donald's legs skittered over cobblestones. In his panic he hardly noticed where they were going. They hurried through a maze of narrow streets taking him far from Bayram's house. Donald looked desperately for anyone who might aid him. His bound wrists upset his balance. Each time he stumbled, the pistol pushed against his neck forced him to lurch on.

As they rounded a corner in a strange neighborhood, he heard a single German word. A Leopard tank lumbered down the street. Standing in the open hatch was a blond soldier.

"I'm American teacher," Donald shrieked in German.

His captor jerked him around and smashed him in the mouth with the pistol, warning, "Not another word out of you."

The gun pressed against his neck again. "Move!"

The German KFOR soldier looked quizzically after the pair disappearing into the gypsy quarter. Several of the houses were reduced to skeletal remains like something from World War Two. Firecrackers or gunshots that had been distant before were close and loud.

On they went, reaching Tusus, an Albanian borough Donald had never visited. White conical hats multiplied around them. Under each he hoped to see Agim's brown eyes. A man crossing the street was the right size. Seeing Agim's market bag on his arm, he called out, "Agim!"

Just then, Donald was jerked off the street into a low corridor. Each step away from the public street was more fateful, taking him further from any hope of rescue. Blood was oozing across his teeth. The taste on his tongue increased his panic. Did Agim see him? Confusion and fear so permeated his mind he could imagine anything.

The corridor ended at a door. A spy hole opened. A dark wild eye fixed fiercely on him, then shifted to his captor. The door banged open and Donald was shoved through it. Behind it were two more UCK soldiers.

"Another one? Where's his house?" The wild-eyed one had a pistol in the holster under his armpit, close to

Donald's face.

"I'll be back," Donald's captor responded.

Donald tripped up two steps and was thrown through a door. He landed face down on the floor. The door slammed closed. The lock rattled with a finality that suggested long imprisonment.

Blood splattered the walls above him and mixed with excrement on the floor. There were unwanted and unidentifiable sour odors. He closed his eyes on the fetid room, exhausted and frightened. *Only Agim, if Agim it was, could know I'm here.*

The emptiness was broken by a long drawn out sigh that sounded like, "Allah!"

19

There was someone else in his cell! Donald's eyes flew open.

Across the gloomy cell a figure bent forward on the floor. Donald tried to stand but his ankle refused, sending sharp pain waves. He crawled on elbows and knees toward the pudgy figure. The man was kneeling with his face almost touching the concrete floor. His wrists were bound together behind his neck. A feathery fringe was matted around his bald pate. Deprived of his fez, his profile was a stranger's. Only the brown velvet jacket straining across the short plump arms was familiar.

"Bayram!" Donald choked out, recognizing his friend. "What are you doing here?"

"I waited...to tell you… I found it," Bayram gasped.

"Found what?"

"Armenian histories explain Old Iranian."

"Armenia isn't anywhere near Albania." With his own wrists still bound together in front of him, Donald reached out toward his friend's arm. Through a large tear in the jacket, he felt the worn softness of Bayram's favorite shirt of finest Bursa silk. "What happened to you?"

Bayram was gulping for air as though swimming under water, but determinedly continued. "A North Iranian people who arrived in the Caucasus in the third century before the Christian era."

The words outran Donald's mind in the shock of their imprisonment. What is he saying? "The Caucasus? The Caucasus!" Unconsciously he shook his head. "The Albanians couldn't have been in the Caucasus! Boys have taken over your house! How can you talk about linguistics while you're imprisoned?"

Bayram summoned his loudest voice to interrupt, "A North Iranian people." His voice grew fainter with every word. Donald had to lean his ear down close to the floor to hear, "… in the lower Caucasus, along the Kur River until the invasion in 944 dispersed them. The Georgians called Albanians Lek'i and their laws, the codes of the Lek'i. Chechens still have identical codes."

Up on his knees now, Donald leaned forward and tried to lift Bayram's head off the floor. "Who brought you here?"

Instead of answering, Bayram murmured Chechen words adopted in Albanian.

From the street came the rumble of military vehicles, their engines throbbing. Heavy boots came running. There was pounding on a door and shouting in German, "Where's the American?"

In the corridor Donald heard doors slamming and loud arguments. "Find Theqi. The Germans are outside."

The pounding continued until a voice called out in Albanian accented German. "What do you want?"

"We want the American."

The cell door banged open. From behind, Donald was hoisted under each shoulder to waist height. Not letting him stand, his legs dragged helplessly. His backpack slid off one shoulder. Two Albanians pulled him out into daylight, dropped him in the street and darted back into their headquarters.

A dozen crouching German soldiers scrutinized him through the sights of Steyr AUG assault rifles. Two Leopard tanks blocked the street. An armored personnel carrier was parked perpendicular to the sidewalk. Above them a German Huey circled, its rotors ripping the air into a small tornado.

After interminable minutes, two German soldiers stepped out of the personnel carrier and lifted Donald to his feet.

He grimaced as his weight went on his ankle, but ignored it to urge the soldiers, "Wait! My friend is in there. You have to get him out too!"

The Germans exchanged looks that made clear this was not news they wanted to hear.

"Another American?" one of them asked.

"Turkish. Bayram's hurt. You have to release him and maybe others—probably others," Donald pleaded. Two medics began examining him.

Ignoring him, the commander's eyes swept the buildings across the street.

Donald grew insistent, "I saw a lot of blood on the walls. Very little of it came from Bayram."

"We'll have two hundred Turkish troops here next week," the intelligence officer informed his commander, "looking out for the Turkish population here and in Dragas and Mamusa."

The blue veins in the commander's temple pulsed. "We'll have to get the Turk out." He turned to another officer, "Call for reinforcements to control this intersection. Get this building cleared. I don't want our friends getting agitated. Very calm. No excitement. I want the American gone. Out of Prizren. Out of Kosovo."

The German calling for back up was off the phone. A second German helicopter roared into view overhead, whipping up the litter in the street.

While the medics cleaned, medicated and anesthetized his lip, Donald strained to hear the commander shouting into the noise. Unseen hands lifted him up into the personnel carrier. He held a rip-open cold pack on his lip with his left hand. More cold packs were taped around his ankle.

"What about Bayram?" he called out to no one in particular from inside the empty vehicle.

"I'm sorry to tell you, he had a heart attack. You're going to Macedonia."

Donald grabbed the frame of the personnel carrier and started to stand up. "Let me see him."

Young soldiers piled in around Donald and they took off.

20

A battered old Yugo came bouncing and swerving down the deserted street toward the German checkpoint. Singing and shouting, the passenger waved a bottle out his window. Steering with his elbows, the driver joined in the chorus, firing his shotgun at the sky.

All afternoon gunfire suffused the city. This time the Germans reacted. Sharp cracks erupted from a dozen assault weapons pushed against their slings. Puffs of gray powder burst off the concrete wall where pretty Albanian girls once gathered to lean over the river or flirt with Serb soldiers. As the dust fell to the ground and the air cleared, the wall was newly pockmarked.

German KFOR shooters blew out the tires. The bottle flew out of the passenger's hand. The windshield shattered. The driver and passenger jerked. The yellow Yugo skidded to a stop in front of the wall. A trail of oil marked its path under attack. The driver slumped over the wheel, immobile. The passenger fell out of his door, tracking his rakija bottle. He dragged himself a few feet, calling for help.

His pleas became unintelligible grunts in between phrases of "Fog fell upon the Bojana."

    The lethal song seemed familiar. Donald was too disoriented to recognize the drunken version before it distilled into wordless moans. The pool of blood spread out around his wretched face to pavement death. *Where I first set foot in Kosovo. Yes, there is the newsstand behind him, a few yards from where I got off the bus.* Studying his face, Donald thought he recognized a farmer who sold turnips beside the river. *Did he sell turnips where he bleeds to death?* Donald's mind could not absorb what his eyes and ears took in. The day's fragments shattered into incoherence.

    Blood oozed out of the Serbs. The German medics needlessly replaced the packs on Donald's ankle several times. Ambushed by the calm authority of their indifference to the dying men, he remained spellbound in dread and horror, never venturing beyond a worthless silent reprimand. The half-hour it took the old Serbs to die seemed an eternity of guilt and failure from inside the armored personnel carrier. Looking away he saw a boy scrawling words on the wall. Morte i Serbi. Death to the Serbs.

    "There's the shuttle from Macedonia. Get him on it."

    Aid workers piled out near the German checkpoint, unloading their supplies. A young German soldier put Donald on the bus. It was heading back to Macedonia to bring in more aid for refugees returning with breathless speed.

An officer leaned into the open door of the bus. "Go home," was all he said to Donald. Then he impatiently waved off the bus.

Holding onto the overhead racks as the bus climbed the hill leaving Prizren, Donald tried to see the old men on the pavement. He lurched down the aisle but they were out of sight. Dropping his pack onto a seat, he slumped down beside it. Being the only passenger gave him an uncomfortable sent-home-from-school feeling. When he arrived the bus had been full and slipped into Kosovo while he had been too immersed in conversation with Agim to notice the border. Now the bus was empty and he had been the sole focus of the new authorities, the German forces that rescued him. The two bus rides were the bookends of his quest. He had arrived filled with excitement and optimism. Leaving, he was a haggard defeated retiree, alone with too many deaths.

To push away the anguish, he desperately grasped the chore of recreating the list of Old Iranian words from his lost notebook.

Banda, meaning band, closed, marked off, is the source of many Albanian words, including: banat (ward, district), bândë (line, row), bandizuom (outcast, exile, banished).

His mind was preoccupied with the anomaly and refused to recall other roots Bayram had told him. How did these words find their way into the Albanian language? Hop-skipping across countries and regions of the globe to land in the mountains of Albania and nowhere else in the Balkans? *A North Iranian people—could it possibly be true? They emigrated west in the tenth century. Hhmm. That could explain the Thracian tattoos. It fits with the first records of them in the Balkans in the eleventh century. Bayram said Georgians called the Albanians the Lek'i and their laws, the codes of the Lek'i. The origin of Leke! The Kanun of Leke, the codes of Leke! Your discovery, Bayram!*

Finding another connection, he blurted out loud, "Living along a river that flowed into the Caspian Sea, the Kur. And Kur, meaning larder, which the Kur River was for whoever lived there. And Kuran, salmon trout! Those were Albanian words that didn't fit anything I was looking at. I go off hunting for the origins of Albanian, and Bayram finds all of this without leaving his house!" Donald began writing the Chechen words in Albanian.

jigit, the Chechen heroic rogue who flies out of the mountains to rob or attack is jezít, the Albanian admirable rascal

It was a research triumph but a terrible one. He wanted the Albanians to be Illyrian. Donald felt drained, betrayed by no longer innocent academic inquiries. Yet his mind pursued the new idea even as he resisted it. *It may fit all the evidence we have. All I ever found in the Vatican libraries were those first communications from the head of a clan in Albania inquiring about the Latin Church.* The two missives arrived at the beginning of the thirteenth century from an author familiar with the Eastern Church centered in Constantinople. They suggested he was a recent arrival in Albania.

With the discipline of decades of scholarship, he bent over his list, scribbling the case that would disprove his own cherished theory. Only when he had filled half a dozen pages, did he notice the acrid smell of the prison floor on his trousers. It brought back the horror of Bayram's bowed figure.

He stopped writing.

Outside the dirty bus windows, an old church caught fire in an empty village. Wood exploded in red-hot splinters flying into the air above the houses, waving a sad farewell of flaming handkerchiefs as he passed. Methodically torched, the villages were rising up in columns of smoke, forming a gray canopy across the sky. Kosovo thundered since the evening he arrived. Now it was burning.

Prizren had been his Ottoman delight but strangers had displaced Bayram from his house and the precious Ottoman records were swiftly disintegrating in the sun and water, never to be read again. The land Donald had known for seventy-eight days was disappearing forever in chaos and death.

Ahead of the bus and behind it was a long line of cars, all leaving Kosovo. Every one of them had furniture and appliances tied on the front, back and sides in high precarious piles. They traveled down the middle of the road or veered from side to side, dodging potholes, gullies and bomb craters. The diesel laboring of the bus recalled the deep chords of Rachmaninoff, slowly, sadly moving up, gaining ground with difficulty. When he heard it coming from Café Zlatni Papagaj, it seemed lyrical. Today he felt only the underlying melancholy of the composer.

A shallow bridge crossed a stream as the rising complex harmonies of several measures began with a fortissimo arpeggiated chord. Beyond the stream, a farm was going up in flames. The squeals of pigs roasting alive in their sty broke through the crashing of timbers as a roof collapsed. Mist rolled down the Cruel Mountains, hiding crimes from the world.

Impatient with the creeping pace of traffic, the bus driver pulled over on the rough and began passing cars. The license plates peeping out below the bulky bundles were from Italy, Switzerland, Germany, and Austria. Each car had only one occupant, the driver, wedged in beside more loot, his knees up to the steering wheel and his forehead almost at the windshield. At last the solid line of cars turned off to the Albanian border, leaving the bus alone on the Macedonia road. The Moment Musical fell through dissonant chords as the bus accelerated, freed from captivity in creeping traffic.

The last few miles in Kosovo were accompanied by a final repetition of the theme in a simple series of treble notes. The plaintive notes recalled the distressed cries of the drunken Serb who lay dying on the pavement. The music in his mind was Kosovo's funeral dirge for the ill-success of his Albanian quest. Unwilling to accept their import, he left the lists of words behind in Kosovo

21

Pec, Kosovo June, 1999

As the tinkle of cups on a tray passed Leposava, she smelled Turkish coffee. She opened her eyes on two dirty linen sacks.

Beyond them were roses. Her eyes searched for the deep cups of crinkled pink petals surrounded by green fringe, the Chapeau de Napoleon. Delicate and diminutive, its mossy lace enclosed the bud, then retired below the opening blossom as it released its deep perfume.

Those weren't her grandmother's roses and she wasn't in her garden. But where?

A heavy gate shrieked as it closed across a stone threshold. A nun secured it and returned across the garden. Behind the gate, keeping the surrounding threats at bay, Italian soldiers called "Grazie."

Leposava remembered someone talked about Italian soldiers. *I know that gate. It's —it's Pec. Why am I in Pec?*

A nun carried the tray of cups past her again. This time there was no coffee aroma.

Leposava lowered her gaze from the sun's glare to the

bags in front of her. Through the soiled fabric she recognized the shapes of Petar's childhood opanci. The curtains, so freshly ironed and clean when she put them up on her kitchen shelf were now bloodstained and wrinkled. They bulged with all she could gather in a desperate rush. The familiar outlines of Pantalone, Arlechino, Columbina and the others shaped the soiled linen in barely perceptible bumps and ridges known only to her.

And the lovers, where are they?

It was hard to make sense when she couldn't remember. Disjointed snatches of the morning came back in slow motion. *I did take those bundles to the road.* Leposava could still hear the thrashing of the wings beating the air before the eagles and buzzards whirled and swooped down toward the bloody flesh that drew them. *Under the shadow of the dark wings I waited for the white van.*

Rocks rained down on the van in the ravine. One crashed though a window. A new volley shattered all the glass. The door jerked open. The driver cursed as he was dragged out and beaten by a screaming mob. Shots rang out. Four hands held her head and shoulders as a rock cracked against her head.

Like a sleepwalker awakened out of place, she had lost her moorings. How could she reassemble that day's bloody mosaic? Around her, in the Patriarchate of Pec were others from the van. Beside the fountain a man who looked to be 100, told someone, "The wrong first caller on Bozic can bring bad luck to the house. Our visitor was bad and see what a year we've had!"

"We left behind our harvest," said his neighbor's wife.

A bee came buzzing, leisurely visiting rose after rose. There was something she needed to remember about the roses. They grow beyond the stump. That stump, and the tree before it, which had shaded and protected her family through hundreds of years in Metohija. The stump that held her harvest of rose petals. The stump where he sang and bowed his gusle, or chopped wood for the stove. Chopped. She heard again the brutal tattoo of strange boots on her kitchen floor. Then her eyes and mouth were covered.

The picture of Petar returned, unwelcome. She tried to force the bloodied tree stump from her mind. That stump she saw this morning covered in a river of red flowing from Petar's headless body. And on it, sitting where Petar's head should be, the falcon of his broken gusle. His songs were silenced.

She could not see her roses with that awful stump before her. She closed her eyes and lowered her head back onto her bundles. Against her cheek she felt the stiff mustache of Pantalone, strong, so unbroken, after all the decades and history of this century in Metohija. She had put him with the other figures on the little tree for Badnji Dan. The snow had come and in the morning Petar drove them in the sleigh through a white world to Zociste.

"It was only a harvest of tears," another neighbor said.

Striking a chime, a nun moved through the garden and into the Church of the Holy Apostle. Singing reverberated out the door around and above Leposava, whispering protective echoes from the thirteenth century. She pushed herself to her feet. Serbian soil still held her up. Putting the bundles over her shoulder, she went to the gate.

A black robed figure ran up behind her. "Leposava, Leposava! What are you doing?"

"Harvest," she said.

"Italian reinforcements are coming with a new bus to protect you and take you to Montenegro. It won't be much longer. Come into the church where it is cool. The sun is so bright out here it's disorienting. In there you won't hear the gunshots or see the rocks come over the wall."

"Montenegro? No." Leposava repeated, bewildered. "I'm going home." She raised the latch and passed out of sight.

GLOSSARY

babica = a Serbian midwife

Badnji dan = Serbian Christmas Eve on Jan 6

Besnik Citaku = character from other volumes of the trilogy, a cousin of Byteqi's father

Bistrica = the river through the center of Prizren

Bozic = Serbian Christmas Day on Jan 7

bourek (Serbian) or **burek** or **börek** (Turkish) = a kind of pie made with spinach or cheese or ground meats

Bundesvier = German armed forces

Christian taxes = collected from the Serbians who refused to convert to Islam under Ottoman rule

cifut = Albanian word meaning Jew or coward, interchangeably

darbuka = Turkish goblet shaped drum played with fingers

DM = Deutschmark, the currency of Germany

Dinar = Yugoslav/ Serbian currency

domazet = a Serbian man who goes to live in the house his wife has inherited. Often he adopts his wife's household slava

Drenica = zone of western Kosovo under the KLA commander Ramush Haradinaj. "Send to Drenica" or "Issue papers for Drenica" was the order for KLA execution.

FARK = Forcat Amatosur e Rpublikes se Kosoves = a guerrilla group rivaling the UCK/KLA, based in northern Albania

gheg = the older form of Albanian spoken by remote mountain tribes and in Yugoslavia until the end of the twentieth century

Grand Vizier = the head of the temporal government in the Ottoman Empire

guslar = Serbian ballad singers who traveled from court to town, accompanying their songs on a gusle

gusle = a one or two stringed instrument portrayed in Serbian novels of the 14th century and played by Kings, outlaws and peasants alike. It is both plucked and bowed.

hararet = the large central chamber of a Turkish bath

Illyrians = ancient non-Indo-European people who inhabited Slovenia, Herzegovina, Montenegro and northern Albania. To combat their piracy in the Adriatic the Romans launched Illyrian wars in 229BC and 219BC.

kanun = Albanian traditional codes governing all legal and social aspects of their lives

kefiyeh = scarf headdress wrapped around head and twisted to fall over the shoulder

KFOR = Kosovo Force, the peace-keeping operation in Kosovo after the war

khedive = the Ottoman name for the card game bridge which they invented

KLA = Kosovo Liberation Army

Kosmet = shortened version of the name Kosovo- Metohija

Kosovo Polje = the plain of the blackbirds in Serbia, adjacent to Metohija.

Krsna slava = Christian slava, the celebration of the household saint

KSK = German Special Forces, elite units like the US Delta Force.

kumbar = Albanian godfather, from the Serbo-Croatian Kum and

Greek koumbaros

Kumovo Kolo = Godfather's Round Dance

Lapse = impolite Albanian name for gypsies

lugàt = Vampire

Metohija = the land of the priories (Serbian) was the name on medieval and later maps of Kosovo. Much of Kosovo was owned by the orthodox monasteries, churches and hermitages until Tito expropriated their lands. The name is still in use either as Kosovo and Metohija, or Kosmet.

MUP = Ministry of Internal Security police, the intimidating Yugoslav federal force developed and trained by Slovenian Stane Dolanc for Tito and his successors.

Ottoman rule = various parts of Serbia were conquered by the Ottoman Empire at different times. Prizren was under Ottoman rule longer than the rest of Serbia.

pillion = seated behind the rider on horse or other beast of burden

qeleshe = white egg-shaped felt hats worn by older Albanian men, also called plis

raki = Turkish anise flavored aperitif

rakija = Serbian brandy

roker, rokerski, rokeri = rock stars, rock bands and rock fans in Serbia

Rahman Morina = the Albanian head of the Kosovo Police under Tito and long time Chairman of the League of Communists in Kosovo

salep = milk is cooked with the powdered root of Turkish forest orchids to make a hot aromatic winter drink

SAS = British Special Air Service, commandos trained to operate in harsh conditions from mountains to desert, similar to the US Delta Force. They identified bombing targets operating inside Kosovo near borders.

Siptari = a slang Serbo-Croat term for Albanians which is based on a word Albanians use

staresina = the head of household in an old-fashioned Serbian zadruga. The position was inherited but maintained by consensus.

Sublime Porte = an exalted portal or gate, the translation of the title of the Ottoman government in Istanbul including the Grand Vezir and his Council of State

tosk = When Enver Hoxha, the leader of Albania, had a standard written Albanian created in 1972, he used Tosk because that is what he spoke growing up in southern Albania. Pristina University later adopted the Tosk Albanian textbooks Albania produced.

UCK = Ushtria Clirimtare e Kosovës = KLA = Kosovo Liberation Army

virgin honey = the first harvest of a new hive or a new swarm of bees

VJ = Vojiske Jugoslavij = Yugoslav army

yufka = thin unleavened Turkish flat bread

zadruga = a traditional Serbian communal farming compound based on blood relations

Zlatni Papagaj = Golden Parrot, the name of a popular rock club that opened in Belgrade in the Milosevic era. Also the most famous Serbian rock song by Elektricni orgazam, which was launched with a music video filmed at the club.

SELECTED DATES

229 and 219 BC   Rome's Illyrian wars to suppress piracy in the Adriatic Sea

1459 – 1913   Kosovo-Metohija was within the Ottoman Empire, following a decade as a vassal state

winter of 1915-1916   Following the Austro-Hungarian invasion of Serbia, the Serbian Army defended Kosovo on three fronts until they retreated in front of the Bulgarian sweep across the province.

1941   Nazi Germany invaded Yugoslavia. Kosovo-Metohija was occupied by Mussolini's Italian forces.

24 March, 1999 7pm GMT   NATO launches cruise missiles against FRY from US & UK warships in the Adriatic, the opening of 78 days of bombing Serbia. First targets included the police headquarters in Djakovica. Because of the Turkish population or the historic architecture or both, Prizren was not bombed during the first month of the war. After that only the Roma district was bombed.

June 3, 1999   Kosovo Peace Plan, followed by Serb soldiers' withdrawal from the province and KFOR occupation of Kosovo

June 12, 1999   Russians took the Pristina airport and KFOR arrived in Kosovo

FURTHER READING

For those nterested in reading about the war these books and reports will lead you to many more.

Prizren under the Ottoman Empire:

"The minaret of the principal mosque is a wooden pepper-box, but it has for base a broad stone tower; behind the tower rise the five cupolas of a church. The portico of another mosque rests on pillars torn from an adjacent monastery, and the stones still bear the sign of the cross."

"From these eminences to the further end of the glen is a journey of four hours, which would bring one to the village of Belaï, now Albanian, but containing the ruins of a small Serbian convent and a cemetery with four hundred [Serbian] graves. Between this village and the monastery of Detchani the sides of the glen are perforated with hermitages, little chapels, and cells, half rock, half wall, some still retaining the paintings traced five hundred years ago."

> G. Muir MacKenzie and A. P. Irby, *Travels in the Slavonic Provinces of Turkey in Europe, Volume II* (London: Daldy, Isbister & Co, 1877) 79,103

[Note: when visiting mountain hermitages and chapels between Prizren and Pec, the nineteenth century authors imagined the paintings to be several hundred years newer than the age established by twentieth century scholars and scientists.]

"...the Turks deny the very existence of the Albanian language. The publication of Albanian books is prevented and Albanian schools are suppressed."

Frederick Moore, *The Balkan Trail*
(London: Smith, Elder & Co., 1906) 225

Prelude to the Kosovo War:

On Jan. 13, 1993 Richard Holbrooke wrote a memo to Warren Christopher and Anthony Lake, offering foreign policy advice to the new Administration, including the following goal:
"to punish the Serbs for their behavior...and to brand certain individuals war criminals"

Richard Holbrooke, *To End A War*
(New York: Random House, 1998) 51

"The regional police chief, Mr. Yusuf Karakushi, himself an Albanian who was largely regarded as a Serbian stooge, resigned after the Serbs accused Albanian policemen of failing to protect them and even joining the angry crowd in beating up the Serbs."

Dessa Trevisan, *The Times* (London),
March 27, 1990

"Some UCK operations were apparently intended to drive ethnic Serbs out of their villages. Human Rights Watch heard credible reports of ethnic Serbs being forced to leave the villages of Jelovac, Kijevo, Leocina, Gorni Ratis, Maznik, Dasinovac, Veliki Djurdjevak, Mlecane, Dubrava, Boksic, and Lugodjija."

Humanitarian Law Violations in Kosovo,
(New York: Human Rights Watch, 1998) 75

"Also a serious cause for concern are reports that a number of Serb, Kosovo Albanian and Roma civilians, as well as Serbian police officers, have been abducted since early April by armed Kosovo Albanians, believed to be KLA members. The office of the High Commissioner has interviewed relatives and family members of abductees as well as eyewitnesses to abductions…On 26 and 27 August, in Klecka, 22 persons believed to be abductees reportedly were killed and their bodies burned in a makeshift crematorium."

> Report of the Secretary General Kofi A. Annan to the Security Council September 4, 1998

"Squeezing Out Kosovo's Serbs; None Remain in Several Villages as Ethnic Albanians Extend Their Control"

> Peter Finn, *The Washington Post*, January 4, 1999

[Note: The UNHCR reported that Serbs were ethnically cleansed from 90 villages in Kosovo in 1998 in item 27 of the Report of the Secretary General Kofi A. Annan to the Security Council, January 31, 1999]

"With respect to forced expulsions by the UCK, a case was reported by the OSCE-KVM Regional Centre in Kosovska Mitrovica on 6 February 1999, when a supposed UCK leaflet was distributed 10 days earlier in the villages of Gojbulja/Gojbuja and Miroce/Mirace (Vucitrin), threatening the villagers with violence if they did not leave the areas immediately."

> Kosovo Serbs, Part IV: The impact of the conflict on communities and groups in Kosovo society, Chapter 19, OSCE, 'Kosovo/Kosova As Seen, As Told,' 1999, 'Displaced Serbs,' 4

"Ethnic Albanian guerrillas from the KLA, fighting for independence from Serbia, took five elderly Serbs hostage on Friday in the village of Nevoljane, near the northern Kosovo town of Vucitrin. The ethnic Albanians' Kosovo Information Centre said ethnic Albanian residents of Nevoljane had fled for fear of reprisals."

Andrew Marshall, 'Negotiate over Kosovo—or else,'
The Independent (London), January 24, 1999

[Note: After KLA kidnappings, ambushes or killings, local Albanian civilians fled their villages to avoid Yugoslav inquiry into the crimes or arrest.]

"The group [KVM] was led by an American, William Walker, who had participated in some questionable undercover operations in Central America during the previous decade...the Serbian authorities were suspicious of their overall impartiality, a suspicion that now appears to be justified, based on recent revelations that there was significant CIA participation in the observer force and that valuable U.S. communication and global-positioning equipment was left behind with the KLA when the observer mission was withdrawn prior to the bombing campaign."

Major General (retired) Lewis MacKenzie,
The Ottawa Citizen, March 24, 2000

[Note: Canadian MacKenzie was a peacekeeping commander in the former Yugoslavia.]

"The 'liberated' zones were expanding, Serbian civilians in small but significant numbers were being kidnapped and killed—to encourage stragglers to leave —and arms and ammunition were pouring across the border from Albania."

Tim Judah, *Kosovo, War and Revenge*,
(New Haven and London: Yale University Press, 2000) 156-7

[Note: In the spring of 1998, under western pressure the Yugoslav security service ignored most attacks and the military avoided any involvement. Serb civilians complained they were not protected.]

"Washington and its Western allies, using secret agencies, funded, trained, armed..." [the KLA and ignored the KLA's] "... organized efforts to drive out non-Albanians from Kosovo, to murder moderate Albanian politicians, to intimidate witnesses and judges..."

> Steven Erlanger, 'A One-Time Ally Becomes the Problem,'
> *The New York Times*, March 25, 2001

Casualties during the Kosovo War:

"At least 100,000 and possibly as many as 500,000 Kosovo Albanian men are unaccounted for, raising fears that they may have been killed by Serb forces, U.S. officials said yesterday. ... U.S. officials said there is good reason to presume the worst about any of the Kosovo Albanians reported missing."

> '100,000 Kosovar Albanian Men Missing, U.S. says: State Department report raises fears of Serb slaughter,'
> *The Toronto Star*, April 20, 1999

[Note: Although administration officials suggested 100,000 Albanian men had been rounded up and executed by Serbs in Kosovo three weeks after NATO bombing began, that was simply propaganda as hundreds of investigators determined after the war.]

"The picture that emerged after the end of the bombing looked somewhat different: in Kosovo NATO's bombing had destroyed 13 tanks and killed about 400 Serbian soldiers (an equal number had been killed by the Kosovo Liberation Army), throughout

Yugoslavia anywhere between 500 and 1,400 civilians were killed by NATO bombs—a 'collateral damage' that could be three times higher than the Serbian military casualties; some 2,000 Kosovo Albanians—both KLA fighters and civilians—were killed by Serbian forces after the beginning of the air campaign."

> Introduction by Michael Waller, Kyril Drezov and Bulent Gokay, Editors, *Kosovo: The Politics of Delusion*, (London and Portland, Oregon: Frank Cass, 2001) vii

"The FBI, for instance, conducted two investigations in June and August, 1999. In a total of thirty sites they discovered 200 bodies. A team of Spanish investigators was told that they were going into the real killing fields and should be prepared for the worst. They were warned they might have to prepare 2000 autopsies. They found no mass graves and only 187 bodies, all buried in individual graves."

> Tariq Ali, Introduction, *Masters of the Universe?* (London and New York: Verso, 2000) xvi

[Note: the Spanish forensic team's leader, Juan Lopez Palafox, was unimpressed with what he found in Kosovo as he noted in interviews and articles in El Pais in 2000.]

Ethnic Cleansing Continued in Post-War Kosovo:

"'If you want to destroy an identity, you start with culture,' said Gezim Qendrok director of the National Arts Gallery in Tirana."

> Peter Finn, reporting from Tirana, Albania, *The Washington Post*, May 23, 1999

"Andras Riedlmayer, a Harvard University-based specialist on the art and architecture of the Balkans, says the pillage must be seen as yet another incarnation of the ethnic cleansing ... There are no more Serbs in Musutiste. Almost daily, the houses they fled are being burned, and local Albanians are in no mood to discuss the destruction of the church. A Globe reporter and photographer were detained and questioned by former Kosovo Liberation Army soldiers for taking pictures there, and a roll of film was confiscated."

'Serbs' Kosovo Heritage in Peril',
The Boston Globe, July 30, 1999

"The charges that destroyed it (the church) were placed at just the right spot to bring the whole medieval building down and make certain there was nothing left to rebuild. The Church of Saints Cosma and Damian was built in 1327. It is now a ruin of broken stone, ... scorched pieces of religious icons lie among the ruins. The letters UCK, the Albanian acronym for the guerrilla Kosovo Liberation Army, were painted neatly in white on the wooden doors at the monastery's gate.
The Zociste monastery is one of at least 60 Serbian Orthodox churches and other religious sites that have been looted, burned or, in at least 21 cases, blown up since the NATO-led peacekeeping force, known as KFOR, began to take control of Kosovo..."

Paul Watson, 'Dispatch from Kosovo', *The Los Angeles Times*,
September 22, 1999

"...A dozen Serbian or gypsy homes are burned daily..."

The Washington Post, July 25, 1999

"German peacekeepers detained the 25 guerrilla members and rescued 15 battered Gypsies and ethnic Albanians in Prizren in what they said may be a KLA torture chamber for alleged collaborators. German peacekeepers taking over a police station from the rebels in Kosovo's second-largest city found 15 Gypsies and ethnic Albanians, many of them chained to radiators, most of them bruised and bloody. They also found an elderly man chained to a chair who appeared to have died just before the Germans arrived."

Calgary Herald, June 19, 1999

"The KLA's Commander Drini said the prisoners a mix of Albanians, gypsies and at least one Serb, were criminals. ...The dead man, about 70 years old and not immediately identified, was found beaten and handcuffed to a chair ...'We found many instruments that could be used as torture instruments,' said Lieutenant-Colonel Jeserich, adding these included a club with a chain, sticks with nails and some kind of skewers..."

Bob Roberts, *The Irish Times*, June 19, 1999

"The families of the kidnapped and missing Serbs expressed bitterness because the joint working group of UNMIK UN Interim Mission in Kosovo and the Coordination Center for Kosovo-Metohija has still not started activities to shed light on the fate of the 1,300 kidnapped and the same number of murdered Serbs."

BBC news, December 16, 2001

[Note: the letter sent to Yugoslav President Kostunica concerned Serbian victims in Kosovo in the first year after the arrival of KFOR in June 1999.]

"The device of asking the time to see what language the target responds in has been adopted by Kosovo Albanians—even children—to try to identify Kosovo Serbs remaining in the province. Replying in the Serbian language often leads to harassment or worse."

Laura Rozen, *The Independent,* October 13, 1999

"Valentin Krumov had just arrived in Kosovo, one of the legions of U.N. workers come to help rebuild this devastated land. A Bulgarian, Krumov, 38, attracted the attention of a group of ethnic Albanian teenagers as he took an after-dinner walk with two female colleagues along Pristina's crowded main street Monday evening. Someone speaking Serbian asked him the time, and Krumov replied in Serbian, unaware that he was apparently being put to a kind of ethnic identification test. It was a test he unwittingly failed, and it cost him his life."

Peter Finn, *The Washington Post*, October 13, 1999

"Mihajio Illic, 26, said he's bored to death in Brezovica. But trying to visit his home in Prizren, about 20 miles to the west, is out of the question. 'Probably they will kill me,' he said of the ethnic Albanians in his hometown."

The Associated Press, February 10, 2002

[Note: Brezovica ski resort had $5 lift tickets—too much for the Serb refugees. The US and UN barred their employees from going there as an economic punishment to the Serbs in the enclave. 130 homeless Serbs were squeezed into the youth hostel in Brezovica for several years after they were ethnically cleansed from Prizren in June 1999.]

"One man explained that the best way to set a house on fire was to begin with a pile of paper and cover that with branches. Perhaps embarrassed in front of a foreigner, he then said: 'They burned my house so I'll burn their houses.' Asked why, if his house had been destroyed, he did not move into the Serb house since the owners had fled, he looked incredulous. 'Because one day, they might come back, and then I would have to move out.'"

Tim Judah, Kosovo, War and Revenge,
(New Haven and London: Yale University Press, 2000) 288

"In Pudujevo, British troops mount a twenty-four-hour guard over two remaining Serb grandmothers—'and the Albanians would slot them if we didn't,' a British officer remarks, using a slang term for 'kill.' …It's hard to convey what a chaotic, threatening place the Albanian 90 percent of Kosova is this winter."

Timothy Garton Ash, "Anarchy & Madness,"
The New York Review of Books, February 10, 2000

Made in the USA